the VINE That ATE THE SOUTH

A NOVEL

WRITTEN & ILLUSTRATED BY

J.D. WILKES

Two Dollar Radio
Books too loud to Ignore

Two Dollar Radio
Books too loud to Ignore

WHO WE ARE TWO DOLLAR RADIO is a family-run outfit dedicated to reaffirming the cultural and artistic spirit of the publishing industry. We aim to do this by presenting bold works of literary merit, each book, individually and collectively, providing a sonic progression that we believe to be too loud to ignore.

TWODOLLARRADIO.com

 @TwoDollarRadio

@TwoDollarRadio

/TwoDollarRadio

Proudly based in
Columbus
OHIO

Love the
PLANET?
So do we.

Printed on Rolland Enviro, which contains 100% post-consumer fiber, is ECOLOGO, Processed Chlorine Free, Ancient Forest Friendly and FSC® certified and is manufactured using renewable biogas energy.

 PERMANENT   100%   **BIO GAS** ENERGY   Ancient Forest Friendly™

Printed in Canada

SOME RECOMMENDED LOCATIONS FOR READING *THE VINE THAT ATE THE SOUTH*:

ON THE PORCH. Wilting dixiecrats and debutantes! Guard against "the vapours" whilst lounging in the shade of your veranda and use this book as a fan during those long, hot Southern summers!

BURIED ALIVE? Copies of *The Vine That Ate the South* may also be used as a signaling tool in the event of premature interment. Simply tap the book-spine against your coffin lid in a lively "Morse Code" fashion, lie back, and await rescue!

Pretty much ANYWHERE because books are portable and the perfect technology!

AUTHOR PHOTOGRAPH→ Joshua Black Wilkins

COVER + INTERIOR ILLUSTRATIONS→ J.D. Wilkes

Lyrics in Chapter 21 taken from "Trashy Women" by Confederate Railroad.

Thank you for supporting independent culture!
Feel good about yourself.

Chief Paduke

the *VINE* That ATE THE *SOUTH*

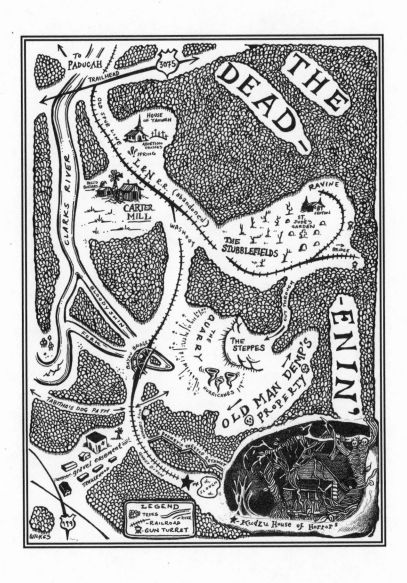

BOOK ONE

THE DEADENING

"To the hard of hearing you shout, and for the almost-blind you draw large and startling figures." —Flannery O'Connor

Chapter One
THE DEADENING

Victims of the Southern Kudzu epidemic.
My friend Carver.
A bike ride to adventure.

Every morning they'd sit beneath the drugstore awning, deal-ing cards and trading fibs, their eyes fixed on the woods across the way. Sometimes their voices would trail off mid-story, as if in a trance. But they'd always snap to with a few good country one-liners:

"Best way to plant Kudzu? Hold it out, drop it, and run!"

"Yup" and "Yessir," they'd answer, staring back into those trees, their voices lowering into a Southern mumble of supersti-tion and slang. In their flannel shirts and WWII VETERAN caps they'd talk for hours, conjuring up an air of mystery. I just hung back and breathed it all in like dark-fired tobacco smoke. It's a place I've always loved, where old warriors told ghost sto-ries and old ghosts told war stories.

"Bless their hearts," said one. "It all just happened so fast."

"Yessir, yessir," they'd answer back again.

Bit by bit, so would assemble my favorite local legend, one

I've heard told by both old and young fogeys alike. A story that goes like this:

A reclusive elderly couple died within days of one another inside their woodland home. Perhaps they were so in love, or so codependent, they just couldn't live apart.

In the resulting abandon, a little Kudzu weed sprouted up through the floorboards. It was nothing more than a sapling, a sprig popping up beneath their bed. But it soon flourished into a monster that filled all four corners of the house. It gobbled up every stick of furniture, every appliance, even the kitchen sink. It got into the chimney; it got into the vents. It even ran down into the plumbing. But that wasn't enough. The vine soon commenced to crave the taste of flesh. So it turned its head toward the deceased.

First it sent but a single strand to weave up their ankles, just for a quick nibble. A toenail here, an earlobe there. Just a taste. Then it gathered itself up, burgeoning under the bed where the two lay spooning. It spread out wide, climbed the ceiling, and curled its tendrils in like the clefs of a lyre. Then with lush abandon, the thing descended to devour them both, stem to stern. It constricted about their torsos, squeezed around their skulls, and sent feelers weaving in and out of every pocket, socket, and hole.

Days passed into weeks. Then months. Soon it began resembling the digesting rat-lumps of a boa constrictor. It gloated and bloated with rich human nutrients and could not be contained. The rate of its growth doubled, then tripled. It pulled itself evermore through the floorboards like a giant thread unraveling from the very fabric of Nature.

At last, it burst through the walls and overtook the entire Kentucky cliff-top. Plus anything else in sight.

Since the shut-ins had no family to remove what was left of their bodies, the plant reserved the honors for itself. And in the same way an acorn can fall to the earth and spring to a mighty life of its own, in the same way roots exhume the coffins they so rudely invade, this humble weed defied expectation. It gathered the lovers up, pulled them through the window and crocheted them into the wilderness.

To this day, so it is said, it's all there for anyone to see: a horrible hillbilly filigree of dangling belongings and shocking remains. All of it cocooned in the oaks up on high.

Yes, for decades these souls have just hung there, caught in a gauzy blur between Heaven and Earth. Robes of flesh fell away as a new circulatory system twisted through their bones. It is said that the husband, in particular, suspends crowned with the graying laurels of past winters. His jaw hangs like a swinging crescent as his ribcage houses a nest of squirrels. And his skull-eyes are the doors of a martin gourd.

But as well known as the old dead couple is down here at the drugstore, the truth is that few have actually laid eyes on them.

A collective belly-laugh at some corny joke always signaled the start of their slow, moseying dispersal.

"Whelp, fellers. Keep the shiny side up and the greasy side down." Or, "Whelp, fellers. Glad ya got to see me!"

You couldn't leave until you heard a quip and chuckled. Then off they'd limp out from under the awning toward their farm trucks to sputter home, thinking no more of the Kudzu House and the poor couple that hangs outside.

But as for me, myself, and I, we aim to find them!

KENTUCKY

The "Old Spur Line" is the name of the abandoned railroad bed that cuts a path directly toward this mortal coil of legend. Both the railroad and the house—plus the sea of trees that swallows them both—can be found in the western swamplands of Kentucky. Our eight little counties have little to no violent crime to speak of, transfixed as we are on our lazy rivers. It is a place utterly cut off from the rest of the commonwealth. Almost an island unto itself.

It is called the "Jackson Purchase." That's because President Andrew Jackson, Old Hickory himself, huckstered it away from the Chickasaw. Local native Chief Paduke, who may or may not have really existed, was swindled out of his land too, done in by George Rogers Clark, kin to those "Lewis and Clark" guys. This area shares borders with other local castoffs: the "Bootheel" of Missouri and a sad section of Southern Illinois known as "Little Egypt."

The Jackson Purchase shares the same line of latitude as Damascus, Yokohama, and the Rock of Gibraltar, but there are few topographical highlights. Only the occasional Appalachian foothill can be seen here or there, subducting into the trench of the Mississippi River and descending out of sight forever into the underworld.

HOW TO FIND THE OLD SPUR LINE

Go to the Littleville Bottleworks and cut to the left. There's an empty schoolhouse where kids break in to steal old flags and maps. Head around back. Here the Old Spur Line begins its way into Marshall County, crooked as a dog's hind leg. This is the trail that leads us to our dark prize, the Kudzu House of Horrors. Soon our journey will begin and we shall see the mythic Gordian Knot. A Kong-size monkey fist clenching real human skeletons!

HEXEN

I am drawn to the forest today—this instant, in fact. The midsummer doldrums have left me wanting, the weather is nice and the wind is whispering my name. Plus, I have a friend who's supposed to meet me at the trailhead soon.

But a more powerful force beckons me.

It's as if the trees are giant witching rods that lure me in. And why couldn't the woods draw human souls inside? Consider the watchful black-and-white eyes of birch knots and the siren whispers of weeping willows. Come to think of it, aren't both breeds the actual source wood of dowsing wands? As creatures made up of 75 percent water, how can we resist?

And what is our soul but a fluid thing too, a flowing power that tunnels through our veins like currents through underground channels, like the very well-waters sought by the diviner? So, it is obvious! The trees, with their forky sticks a-wigglin', have witched me to their entryway. For I am the well they wish to tap.

COME WHAT MAY

This will be both my first and last childhood adventure, albeit one conducted in my thirties.

Understand, much of my actual youth was spent in a state of arrested development inside a fatherless home. I typically stayed out of the sun, alone in the woods or indoors reading books. I loved anything having to do with Greek mythology, philosophy, the classics, or the Bible. Alas, I am now the type of guy who says "alas."

Yes, there in the dark I'd hide from the hordes of vicious Kentucky hillchildren. As a result, I stifled any desire to tackle the outside world. My innate curiosity was repressed as I hunkered down inside, stuck like a yawn that couldn't be brought to completion.

But not anymore! I have something to prove to not only myself, but to the town. You see, I have a rival in this county. An old enemy who has plagued me since grammar school. Stoney Kingston. He's a loud-mouth blowhard who brags that he's been to see the bodies. Says he left his initials carved in the tree. But I know him too well.

Yeah, he's an impressive guy, with his horse farm, big cowboy hat, muscles and swagger. He stole my One True Love, in fact. Delilah Vessels. However, I aim to prove him a fraud if it's the last thing I do.

Stoney and Delilah (oh, how I hate to say their names together) have been together off and on since junior high. But during one of those off times she was with me. We got Blizzards at the DQ our last visit together. She talked about how she doesn't really love him because he won't commit. How he screws around with rodeo groupies. But two months later they were back at it again, down at the swimming hole, skinny-dipping and you-know-what. Yeah, the whole town told me. Stoney told me too, the bastard. Had the Polaroids to prove it. *Aghhhh*, I don't know. I guess I should move on, but I can't help but think maybe there's hope. Especially if I prove him a fraud, once and for all.

As a grown-up, I have the skills to withstand those old persecutions. Pent-up energy and drugstore legends are fueling a need for excitement. This is the day. I want "to stretch my eyes out" as Grandma used to say when she wanted to see new things. Time to cut loose. No more hang-ups. No more excuses.

I've heard it said: "Dreams don't chase themselves."

CARVER CANUTE

A rusty chain dragging the ground between two posts blocks the trailhead. The upright crossties lean in at one another like an arch missing its keystone. Expert guide and kindred spirit Carver Canute is here, a man fifteen years my senior. He busts off the chain and makes short work of the beams. Barehanded, he bear-hugs each one out of the ground and caber-tosses them fifty feet into a soybean field. It is a completely unnecessary display of strength.

KEEP OUT! NO TRESTPASING!
NO ATV's. NO TRUCK's. NO HORSE's.

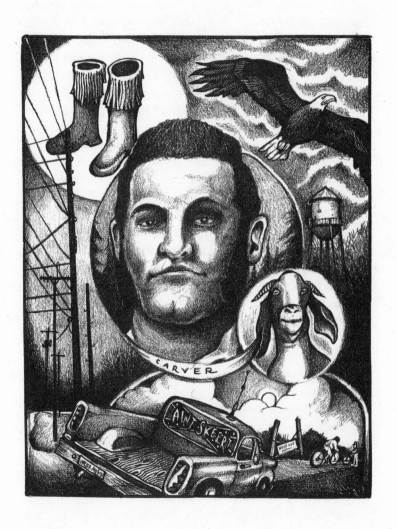

"It don't say a got-dern thing about no mountain bikes."

He puts his boot through the sign, exploding it into toothpicks.

Carver Canute is more ape than man, God love him. He's part hick, part "full-blooded Cherokee." Thunderbolt tribe, specifically. He stands only five-foot-nine but he has all the top-heavy girth of a Minotaur. His shoulders look like football pads, but down at his little hooves he comes to a point like an ice cream cone. And that wild, ruddy head is just the cherry on top.

He's a cocky Elvis-haired hell-raiser who keeps his pompadour aloft with pork drippin's, sweat, and a wafting circle of lies. He's constantly telling whoppers, and he doesn't give a crap what people think about him. In fact, he just left his truck dumped in someone's ditch down the road. It's what he calls his "Holler Mobile," a vehicle that's won MARSHALL COUNTY'S UGLIEST TRUCK CONTEST three years in a row. It's enough to make him display his usual quirk of pride: adjusting the crotch of his pants, as if no pair of jeans on Earth could possibly contain his girth.

But most importantly, Carver is an anachronism. Following a wild spell after his parents died, he was bailed out of juvie and adopted by his Native American granny. Her and her second husband, Zeb Canute. Zeb was a primitive octogenarian hillbilly whose ancestry was "Scotch Arsh." So Carver is a strange combination of both cultures, and a complete generational throwback.

His hands are those of the olde village smithee: broad and calloused beneath a mist of simian hair. Meat hooks really, lacking any flair to express the emotion of speech. They were crafted by God for the sole purpose of upgrading ape to man. Undoubtedly, they could wrench the head off a jackrabbit or make mulch out of most men. His thumbnail is blackened from the wayward hammering of some masculine project. And the meat beneath his skin is permanently toughened from a life of machinery and mayhem. It has left him as oaken and gnarly as an antique cigar-store Indian—as if you could cut him in half, count his rings, and be left in a whiff of disturbed patina.

All in all, he is a good-humored, gear-headed, coon-huntin' raconteur. A thrill-seeking adrenaline junky who sports leather wrist cuffs and a wallet chain. And check out those fringed knee-high moccasins. He calls them his "goatboots."

"Yer suppose't stick their back legs down the front," he tells me. "So they cain't get away, if ya know what I mean."

He has a foul mouth. Literally. I mean, his mouth is foul. It's a veritable monstrance of filth. Specifically, I mean his teeth—or the pea-green excuses he calls his teeth. These hollowed-out stalactites of tar-blotched failure. These bituminous slivers of un-brushed rubbish. These oozing protrusions of pitch, blackened at the gum-line, scaly across the front, smelling of mothballs and decay. All eleven of them (and the George Washington-lookin' three in front) are the remnants of his two-pack-a-day habit. Gawd, he coulda been a star on *Hee Haw*.

I should talk. My sorry gob is held together by three gold caps, an old retainer, and enough lead to cast a set of chess pieces. (They're good for tuning in radio signals at night though!)

The rest of me is rail thin and frail beneath Carhartts, waterproof socks, and galoshes. I am weak and incomplete, the curse of a fatherless home. But I am curious and discerning, cautious yet hungry. Faraway gunshots remind me to put my ball cap on. That Day-Glo orange one that screams, CAUTION! HUMAN HEAD. DO NOT SHOOT!

Between us, we have two canteens, two machetes, a pocket-knife, a compass, a map, and a harmonica I bought at a Cracker Barrel.

Around Carver's neck, hidden under his collar, hangs his grandmother's old "Mad Stone." It's a handy amulet that draws the poison out of animal bites. Only five other Cherokee Mad Stones are known to exist in Kentucky, each supposedly possessing different "magical" properties. My father was obsessed with finding one for himself. We were always stopping at rock shops and junk stores, but all they ever had were hippy crystals and fool's gold. Alas, nary a Mad Stone could be procured.

Carver described how his Stone was once used on the victim of a rabid dog attack. The boy was just four years old when his grandfather left him alone to play on the farm. But mad dogs came, from neighbors away, and descended upon him. A pack of five Rottweilers tore him to shreds.

It was a hysterical scene as everyone on the rez gathered to weep, pray, and sing. Once the doctor got the bleeding to stop, Granny Canute stepped in, Mad Stone in hand, to draw out the disease. A bowl of milk was fetched and the amulet was applied to the wound. Slowly and repeatedly the poison was released from the stone into the bowl, turning the milk a mucus-green. When it finally ran clear, the malady was expelled, and the boy was left alone to mend. And indeed, he grew up strong. He grew up to be Carver Canute!

Whatever else we need, Mr. Canute will show me how to finagle from the woods. He's been to the Kudzu House before and says Stoney is full of crap. It's not an easy place to get to, but Carver makes short work of most obstacles, which is precisely why he's here.

With our ingress made ready, Carver signals the time is nigh. Time to saddle up our ten-speeds, these flat-black spray-painted Schwinns that he probably stole from the "WalMarx."

Ready or not, we hit the trail beneath a purple-soaked, early morning sky.

Chapter Two
GOLGOTHA

The secret history of The Deadening.
A "true" story from Carver Canute.
A failed prophecy.

The Old Spur Line is a whirling portal of living, dead, and living-dead foliage. A forbidden path of Southern mystery, it retreats from our town into the neighboring farm communities. It's a "fur piece" from end to end, as Carver puts it, where the fields are all fallow and the beasts are all feral.

City slickers be warned: the artifices of urban life are absent here. Your whimpers will win you no sympathy. As in olden days, Natural Law is in full swing. Nature, lest you've forgotten, rewards merit and punishes sloth. And, though you may turn a blind eye, a deaf ear, or a cold shoulder, the most barbarian truths are contained in everything you see, hear, and touch.

There are no phone signals either. Only old telegraph lines. But they, of course, are useless. They hang severed or slack from rotten poles, having fallen silent from the chirp of ancient keys. Weather vanes and windmills trace your new skyline, and the only "skyscrapers" here are grain elevators, steeples, and silos.

Curious about our "nightlife"? Try raccoons, possums, and

coyotes. Even wolves are rumored to give chase through the creeping brume of night. Listen close and you'll hear them. They scream, whoop, and holler like a pack possessed by Legion.

The gunplay you hear isn't coming from any of your usual criminals back home. It's actually the sound of those wishing to be self-sufficient. Therefore, whizzing bullets should come as a strange relief. So take it. You'll need as many odd comforts as you can get. Out here you will wander on and on as the path winds and winds. Past places where dancing and public swimming are illegal, where town crests are the shields of boxelders, and Dixie flags flap wild in the wind.

"Does the Dixie flag piss you off?" Carver asks. "The 'rebel' flag, I mean?"

"Why?"

"Well, it orta piss you off. They drawed it up that way. I call it the 'Fuck You' flag."

He says its X of stars forms an angry face that glares right back at you. No longer sagging at half-mast, they fly high down here, beating red as the cape of a toreador, despite a local ban in town. Despite the fact that Kentucky only ever seceded along its southernmost battle lines.

"That red you see, it's from the rebel blood sucked up through the flagpoles. Drawn up from these ol' battlefields. Yup, they bore on down, buddy. True as a Texas derrick! Frackin' straight into them shallow hallow'd graves."

But Dixie-phobes take heart. The Southland is not just some spook house, some bigoted hellhole. Hollywood gives us a bad rap. For the same unsophistication that leads to belligerence and prejudice in some can produce the finest qualities in others. Not far from where the scum of the earth park their trailers, the salt of the earth tend their lawns. The Old Folks at Home.

Their well-watered lawns and smiling dentures sparkle through the honeysuckle. Tidy country homes, complete with tire swings, window boxes, and Astroturf porches, display the health of gentle hearts. Hard work and hospitality are hallmarks of these remaining few. Those who carry on the old traditions.

WILDERNESS

The natural world is the real attraction though. Shadow, mist, and departing starlight, a light wind and the early morning dew. All of it envelops us as we plunge into the phantom serein, seeking our Kudzu House. Locust-chatter and the clickety whir of bicycle gears fill the air. It is a bucolic scene of hope, harmony, and risk.

Carver has told me these woods are known as "Burkeholder's Deadening," named for the old swamp logger who once owned the land.

As the story goes, Old Man Burkeholder went out one day, axe in hand, and "rung" his trees. That is, he felled them by cutting a swath into the bark to bleed them out dead. This makes logging easier for later. The trouble was he himself died before completing the harvest, leaving these morbid mansions standing in vain, hacked to smithereens and now supposedly enchanted.

And so it is said that persons will lose their way in the forest if they are not right with God. Lost and afraid, they will be forced to spend the night, only to escape the next day. Upon exiting, however, one discovers that not just a single day has passed, but an entire year! Carver swears up and down it has happened to him.

His voice is a hoarse gust that pipes forth from his lie-hole. But his twang is charming. You might think he's the type to hassle the skinny likes of me. But, like I said, Carver is too much of a "people person." He's a true conundrum: a Native American redneck who likes music and jokes as much as he likes skinning bucks and running trotlines. Astride his bike, he leads the charge down the rocky way, throwing his head back, popping wheelies, and carrying on about something or another. Some story about God-knows-what.

"Hope we don't get lost in here fer a whole year. I just started seein' this gal from Calvert. Ugly as an ape but she's got some perty tiddies."

DENDROCHRONOLGY

"Lose a year in the forest?" you ask. "Impossible! How could you lose an entire year in one day? What could give a forest power like that?" Well...

As one of the old-timers at the drugstore says, when a man is concocting a scheme he's got his "gears a-turnin'." But he says the same holds true for the oaks, pines, and sycamores of The Deadening. Their "gears" are turning too.

Here's what I think he meant by that.

As you may recall from high school science, tree rings are a sort of sketch of a timeline, one that depicts every year's worth of weather. Fires, blights, inchworms, and other natural causes leave discolorations too. Concentric as the ripples in a pond, they are readily viewable to anyone handy with a crosscut saw.

But here in The Deadening, perhaps there are markings left by supernatural forces as well: things like the Winds of Time, ghosts, and the nightly pelting of stardust. With each passing year, tree rings are riddled with mystic information, like a horoscopic wheel-chart or even an Indian mandala. And once its instructions are received from on high and its pith infused with magic, The Deadening sets its gears to turning, deciphering the details as the years go by and rotating its tree rings like, well, decoder rings.

There's no real way of knowing, but perhaps these wooden circles are more like the inner-workings of a bank safe: free-spinning tumblers that move within one another in opposing directions around a common center. Their notches catch like sprockets until the correct combination is achieved, until the desired results are unlocked.

Whichever way these discs spin inside their bellies, the same old magnetism occurs. And when the time is right, the victims of The Deadening are summoned, and their destinies are meted out in no uncertain terms.

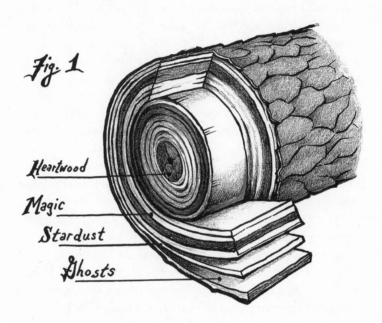

Fig. 1

Heartwood

Magic

Stardust

Ghosts

ARSENIC

We pedal along under the devastation of our strange summer trail. Dead limbs and Kudzu, deer stands and garbage. The air is speckled with gnat clouds, Japanese beetles, and cottonwood fluff. Ahead is a swarm of telephone bugs, the kind that mates late in the season and flies around connected at the gonads.

"You know why they call them telephone bugs, don't ya? Because they say 'hello' and hang up.

"Yep. Well, it's about a three-ire ride from here to that house,"

Carver says, hopping his bike over some fallen limbs. I hop my bike and duck to miss getting a branch in the face.

"Four or five if we gotta do any serious clearin'. But if you go on any farther you'll come to a chain-link fence with all this bob-warr loopin' around top. That's where the government puts all that shit in the warter supply. They do it late at night when everybody's asleep. Fluoride, arsenic, lead. All the stuff that makes it taste like a garden hose. And, brother, that place ain't on no map."

Carver hits the handbrakes. I skid to a halt too, confused by our sudden stop. He pulls a rolled-up Kentucky atlas from his saddlebag and flips it to our county. After scanning the map a few seconds, he points to the exact spot where we stand.

"See. That dotted line is this old railroad grade. And looky what happens."

As I follow his finger to the end, the markings disappear into a void of redacted information. A postage-stamp-size rectangle indicates a vague, generic slough.

"That's a dad-blame lie! I've been there and they's a big ol' government complex with an electric fence, NO TREST-PASSIN' signs, and concertina warr surrounding the whole place like Area 51. They's tryin' to pizen our brains and turn us all into zombies. You'll see it fer yerself by the end of the day! What?! You don't believe me?!" He swats my shoulder hard with his book as if genuinely insulted. His eyes look crazy.

"I believe you," I assure him. Judging from the violent extra emphasis, I reckon I better believe him. Carver adjusts his crotch, mounts his Schwinn, and pedals away, satisfied he's made his point.

Moss and dead leaves overtake the rail bed here. Coal, rusty spikes, and switch-arms poke out of the growth to remind us that this was once part of the great Louisville & Nashville Railroad. But farmers own the land we're on now, so we are technically trespassing. For years this railway serviced the area's main employer, a popcorn factory… before it exploded. I wasn't there but I always imagined the townsfolk coming out to smell the destruction, or to gobble down a few tons' worth of damage.

With no more businesses to serve, the railroad went dark and the government stepped in. They uprooted most of the tracks—though you still see a few lying around—and laid their claim. Except for the occasional civilian plat, the Bureau of Fish and Wildlife currently mismanages most of the forest.

Mr. Canute, as if in an old Western, advises that we "walk softly" until we are back on federal land, where we're less likely to get shot.

Astraddle again and pedaling on for about a mile, we cross from private property to government reserve and then onto sacred ground. A one-room country church squats on brick columns. The watermark of a flood has left a drippy gray plumb line around the building. Many of its marquee letters have blown off in past storms. It just says: *CH–CH*

"What's missing?" Carver asks.

"I don't know."

"U aRe!"

THE COMET

He tells me this is the "House of Yahweh," whose well-house siphons the waters of the River Jordan through a transatlantic tunnel. Believers come from miles around with empty jugs to get their fill of the same waters that baptized Christ. Even hippies believe in the healing properties, describing the well as a sort of mind-spring of Mother Earth, as if Her chambers, like psychic brain synapses, flow with holistic power. But fewer and fewer pilgrimages have been made here lately.

"Brother Stiles built this church… snake handlin' place, it was. But he give up on it a long time ago," Carver explains. "He thought fer sure that Halley's Comet was a-comin' to wipe us all out. Said Jesus tolt him the tail was pizenous and that it was gonna kill everybody in Marshall County. Said it was the curse of an evil Indian spirit."

It's true. I remember watching the reverend try to warn us all on his public access television show. It was one of the many guilty pleasures Delilah and I had, lying in bed on a Sunday morning, eating cold Pop-Tarts and making fun of bad TV. I can still hear her laughing at the preacher's black string tie hanging like a tiny stick-figure body beneath his huge head.

Like a man possessed, he would roll his eyes sunny-side-up behind those horn-rims, babble a bunch of gobbledygook, and erase his blackboard chicken-scratch as quickly as he had just scrawled it, breaking chalk with each lunging new idea. Then he'd stand down the camera. Clench-fisted and pop-collared, he'd scream into that gunmetal microphone as arcane knowledge gushed like black currents. Kindred red springs trickled between the knuckles of his furious fists, mixing with the ink of his sermon notes and star charts, all crunched into a paper wad. I remember them switching to a test pattern so they could stop to bind his wounds.

Delilah just about choked on her breakfast, and, yeah, I laughed along too. But I couldn't shake the notion that he might be right. There was something salient in his prophecy… something familiar in his madness. It greased the creases of my mind like the blood trailed from a copperhead.

"So he packed up his family," Carver continues, "and moved off to Cincinnati and left the church fer his cousin to run. But, hell, that old jasper didn't know nothin' about religion. Next thing ya know, he drunk up all the wine and spent the tithes on pot and porn. The church has been a-settin' there empty ever since."

As we pedal on up, I notice a field of a thousand miniature wooden crosses lined up in rows. It appears to be a mock grave-yard for the unborn. Each little whitewashed cross mimics a miniature Christian marching off to Heaven. A vinyl banner rips in the wind, commemorating the millions of babies aborted each year. In the corner, a cartoon of a weeping Jesus holds a fetus like a pint-sized Pietà.

"What's the difference between a man leavin' church and your mama takin' a bath?" Carver asks.

"I don't know."

"The man leavin' church has a *soul* full of *hope*."

It took me a second.

"Didn't you go to one of them shoutin' churches?" Carver asks.

"Yeah," I seem to recall...

Chapter Three
GODSTORM

Memories of a Christian school.
An exorcism.
Struggles with Faith.

The sun kept an eyeball on me and Mama... a clouded Southern eyeball. It was quiet in the car and I was depressed. It's a lonely feeling starting over at yet another new school.

Much of Marshall County still lay dormant under the few remaining stars of dawn. Mama took the corners slow, careful not to get caught in a speed trap or hit a deer. We had to keep the windows cracked on the Datsun because of an exhaust leak.

On past the DQ and the Western Auto, past the Piggly Wiggly and up to the white A-frame church. She hung a left into the gravel lot where other cars idled, waiting for classes to commence. Dew-kissed windshields fogged like sleepy eyes as they sat parked in a waking coma, anticipating the Gabriel call of the church-school bells.

Fellowship Assembly read the hand-painted sign. A ten-foot red neon cross blinked off and on, and then went dark. Twilight sentinels triggered by the dawning sun.

After Daddy died in "The Accident," it took everything for

Mama not to send her one and only child out into the world wrapped head-to-toe in yellow caution tape. Between her smothering and his absence, I was, and still am, lost when it comes to being a young man. I think too much. I read too much. I draw too much. Hell, I probably register somewhere on the Autism spectrum! But I don't care. I need to get out there and kick some ass, if for no other reason than to get my ass kicked.

Mama told me over and over, "Hush, honey. Never you mind all that. The meek will inherit the earth."

Well, Charles Darwin would disagree. The lord-of-the-flies culture at my high school had only made matters worse for me. They called me "Crap Knife"... I'll tell you about that later, as you'll need time to prepare for such a lovely story.

So Mama, bless her heart, began her search for a Christian school. Apart from the Catholic school (which "would never do"), this was the only other game in town. Fellowship Assembly, an "education ministry" sponsored by an adjoining Pentecostal church, would be my new school. The "campus" was but a single A-frame sanctuary surrounded by three tan mobile homes that served as classrooms. The playground was a see-saw.

BROTHER WITHERS

A man met us at our Datsun and walked me to class. Mama blew a kiss, but I ignored it with feigned independence. As I heard the car pull away, nobody knew I was holding on to every departing pop of gravel under her tires.

"Are you th-aved? Do you know Jesuth?" sputtered my new teacher, Brother Withers. Outside of school, he was known as Mister Withers, the small-town florist with the ironic name.

"Yes, sir," I answered as we walked into a dim room of filing cabinets and boxes. I can still smell the old textbooks, pencil shavings, and chalkboard dust.

"But have you re-theived the gifth of the Holy Th-pirit?" he pressed. His wispy blond moustache did nothing to mask his harelip and "not gay" lisp.

"What are those?"

"Have you ever th-poken in tongth? Have you been fire-baptithzed?" With each question his nervous wink seized with increasing violence.

"No, sir."

"Oh ho-ho-well then!" he sang smugly. "I gueth you've gotta long way to go! The true fruit of God'th favor! The true rewardth of Heaven! You don't even know!"

His chuckle signaled delight in my lost spiritual state. But whatever these "gifth of the th-pirit" were, I wanted to possess them. And this, I was sure, was the kook to show me how!

CHERUBIM

During our praise service at morning assembly, while the pent-a-caustic preacher sang "Jesus" as if it were pronounced "Cheeeese Sauce," I tried my dang'dest to channel these mystical gifts. I even closed my eyes and lifted my hands up in praise like a TV antenna, maneuvering them as if to pull in a better signal. But the harder I tried the worse I failed, and the worse I failed the harder I tried, until I finally peeked to see if anyone was looking at me. No one saw me except some cute girl. She mouthed the word *fag* from across the room.

I started attending the church-school's Sunday services too. I stood in awe as the congregation babbled in tongues like a bunch of chickens. Even small children joined in the fray. One morning the pastor's three-year-old son came and sat beside me. Upon the Invocation, we all stood to praise the LORD. That's when I felt the child's tiny breath blowing hot on the back of my arm as he ululated in the Spirit. This sensation left me shuddering, as if someone were walking over my grave. What is this? How is it possible that this toddler can speak in tongues, but I can't? Surely, there's no need for an innocent kid to be "slain in the Holy Spirit." Then again, consider the following:

> But Jesus said, Suffer little children, and forbid
> them not, to come unto me: for of such is the
> kingdom of heaven.
> —Matthew 19:14 KJV

Yes, but I ask, isn't He the same, unerring One Who inspired our church-fathers to decree an "Age of Accountability"—an exception that pardons children from judgment? Yes, He is the One and the Same. But inconsistency, come to find out, is the name of the game.

Back in homeroom, Brother Withers "suffered" us all. He ruthlessly enforced the dress code, measured my shaggy hair with a ruler, and all but demonstrated how to clench our butt cheeks together correctly.

Corporal punishment was used on full-grown high-schoolers. Public shaming too. He harangued those he thought were "over-sexed" or "wanton," or anyone else who dared voice skepticism. And over and over he insisted, just insisted, that the earth was 4,000 years old and the Devil put the dinosaurs' bones in the ground.

As much a florist of language as he was of lilacs and lilies, Brother Withers arranged verbal bouquets of fear, guilt, and gore. It was one gothic moral lesson after another: first-century martyrs, disemboweled for their faith; medieval saints rectally tortured with iron dildos; sinful souls howling in the agony of Hell; satyr-hoofed demons flaying the flesh of heretics. The student body also felt flayed and left for dead beneath Brother Withers' funeral spray of prose. Suffice it to say, the man was roundly hated by everyone.

Except me. I didn't flinch, lest I miss the slightest pearl of wisdom. I found his gnarly diatribes exhilarating. I ignored what they said about him. Here is a man from whom I could learn the secrets of the hidden world.

REVIVAL

Indeed, among the church congregation, Brother Withers was a superstar. I witnessed him in full Southern gospel mode at a three-day weekend revival. The Reverend Cecil Tazewell's Traveling Ministry!

Yes, the right Reverend Tazewell! He was the fast-talking, Brylcreem-ed charlatan on a "Crusade for Christ." He delivered the powerful Saturday night sermon that conveniently doubled as a commercial for his spray cans of "Miracle" aerosol. Yep. If the Devil's in the details, this reverend was into retail!

But his sales pitch was preceded by a sideshow. THE SAMSON BROTHERS POWER TEAM MINISTRY. Five adrenaline-crazed bodybuilders straddled the stage, tweaking on Jesus and perhaps crystal meth. With Clydesdale hooves, inappropriate bulges, and chiseled thighs clutched in perma-flex, they tore through phonebooks and screamed in fake Hebrew through their headset microphones. But CBers kept breaking in over their signal, filling the sanctuary with profanity and trucker slang.

"Breaker Breaker! Where's all them neckid wimmen out there?! Come on back to Big Red!" hollered one trucker.

"Shut up, stupid!" came the reply.

"Go to hell, Muff Diver! I gotcher 10-20. I know where you live!"

"Bring it on, shit-for-brains!"

Tazewell quickly stepped in and saved the moment, commencing his sermon over a hard-wired microphone.

He recounted the plight of a married couple that had driven their dead daughter to his home. They had traveled cross-country some 2,000 miles in the summer heat. And, despite the smell, you can be sure that Tazewell most assuredly gave them the miracle they were hoping for. The Good Reverend had raised the dead!

The crowd gasped. Brother Withers leapt, wept, and shouted things like "Hallelujah!" "Mustard Seed Faith!" and started going into convulsions. He hopped up on a church bench and ran pew-back to pew-back to the front of the cheering multitude. Upon reaching the first row, he jumped off, rode the Rev piggyback, and executed a perfect back flip into the baptistery. It was spectacular. The feverish throng of believers rejoiced as Brother Withers sloshed in the hog trough of holy water. A-splashing and a-singing and a-shouting. Why, with the way they were all carrying on you'da thought that tub had been filled with the very hemoglobin of Christ Himself!

At one point, five hours later into the "Godstorm" (the hip youth-pastor term for a revival), Brother Withers even appeared to levitate a few inches off the ground. I saw it with my own eyes! As a result, the place went nuts. The Altar Call drew in dozens and the revival endured for a full three months more, eventually spilling into a tent outside. Scores of souls would be saved and hundreds of cans of Cecil Tazewell's aerosol "Spray Blessing" would be sold.

EXORCISM

Church services went back to normal after Tazewell drove his little blue campervan back to Gibsonton, Florida, the place where carnies famously winter. Strangely, Brother Withers did not show up to teach the next semester. His only daughter, a fellow student in my homeroom, had gotten pregnant over the summer break. But she was not expelled. Not yet at least. Rather, she was suspected by the elders of having become possessed by an evil spirit: a local "demon of lust" known as Crypteroticles. I only know this because, while at school, I stumbled in on their little mid-morning exorcism.

I had been sent by my math teacher to retrieve a stapler from the principal's office. To get there, I would have to pass through the sanctuary. But just as I extended my hand to open the church door, it violently threw itself wide, causing me to leap back. After a curious squint, I slowly stepped inside.

Once my eyes adjusted to the dark red-glassed inner sanctum, I beheld six men in deacon suits, holding down the supple bucking body of a teenage girl. Each was performing an ad-libbed ritual as she flailed on the floor, cussing in tongues. Sure enough, the demon's own signature, full of crooked symbols and zigzags, had been scrawled across the pulpit in blood.

CℛYP+ℯℐOℐℳCLEs

The men were shouting in the Spirit and dousing her school-girl shirt with anointing oil. Well, it was really just a bottle of Wesson. "Kentucky-Fried Christian" grease.

"In the name of Jesus we rebuke thee!" came the command as the musky circle of men rotated around her body, slinging oil while I stood watching. Heavy breathing from a hot, heaving body; sweat-kissed breasts; rolling, whorish eyes; the lolling tongues of men and angels. But each prayer elicited only moans and more sensuous movement upon the floor. In retrospect, it sounds more like an orgy.

"Um, I'll just be in here getting the stapler," I muttered and hurried on toward the supply room. (Should children really ever have to walk in on an exorcism at school?)

Days after, the whole town learned that Brother Withers had committed suicide, so ashamed was he of his befouled daughter. His "Altar ego" so wounded.

Word was he had trudged to the outer edges of The

Deadening, locked himself inside the loft of a dark-fire tobacco barn, and suffocated on the smoke.

It is said that he was last seen through the busted louvers of the cupola, his silhouette writhing against the orange setting sun. The old-timers down at the drugstore said they also saw the outline of "skeletons dancing" around his body. And the daughter, who was later expelled, reportedly gave birth to a "kiddy pool of serpents."

So there I was, robbed of another father figure. Alas, Brother Withers' last tent revival was to be the blue rain-soaked canopy of his graveside service.

It would be my final one too, as the remainder of my adolescence concluded without his tutelage. I never received the gift of glossolalia (AKA "speaking in tongues"), I never "laid on hands," and I never cast out devils. Woe is me. My fire-crowned Day of Pentecost never came.

DISMISSAL

A decade or more has passed and, thanks to the wisdom and retrospect of adulthood, I have given up. I have kept my faith but suspended the bulk of my religion, determining that "tongues" is nothing more than the unfettered id of the simpleminded faithful. It is the panicky cluck of repressed farm-folk who are at a loss for words to express their anxiety. So it's not magic, it's manic. Put yet another way, tongues is like spiritual scatting. Like jazz for Jesus. And holy-rollin'? Well, that's just a punk rock show for God.

Let me be clear: I don't begrudge anyone their manner of worship. (Better to engage in charitable gatherings than to surrender to the nihilism of our Industrial Complex.) But, understand, this is where I come from and who I am. Forget nagging doubts. Nagging religion can be worse. Every natural impulse is questioned, every human desire squelched by the Kudzu-like growth of religiosity as it strives to fill in all gaps of understanding.

Having said that, I still love God. He's the only daddy I have now. But I trust these woods are no different than anywhere else I've traveled since graduating from Fellowship Assembly. North, south, east, and west, everywhere it's the same scene:

A thousand and one little jesuses judging, whining, scrutinizing, scuttling under the branches, creeping in the ditches, and peeping out the gopher holes. Come what may, I will face them all as I tackle this day in The Deadening, terrible, swift machete in hand. Because I shall always be a man in search of hidden truth.

"Yeah, I went to one of those churches for a while," I say to answer Carver's question.

"Well, I hain't goin' to Heaven or Hell when I die. I'm gonna come back as a poltergeist. You know, like in that movie? Anyway, right up cheer is Carter Mill."

He starts pedaling faster. Faster than I can keep up with. I pop the derailleur and stand up to pedal.

"You've got to see it," he hollers. "It's an honest-to-goodness ghost town!"

Chapter Four
HUMBUG

Vampires.
A Mystery Pitchman.
Eerie noises in a ghost town.

Not all tree limbs grow toward the sun. Cowering from the sunlight, the boughs of The Deadening curl over us like claws. Dozens of snapped limbs hang straight down, connected at the elbows by weakening strands of wet bark, the result of an old ice storm. They point down like stalactites, or "widow-makers" as they call them—so named for their tendency to break off and impale you while you walk underneath. I find myself holding my breath. The dangling branches remind me of the sleeves of scarecrows, hanging baggy off their armsticks. And the wind is currently making them pendulum like a vaudeville comedian's broken arm.

Beavers have dammed up the gullies. Their clay-caked huts block entire sections of the river into standing black pools. The little critters are laboring just feet away as Carver and I stand in awe of our World. What peaceful solitude and grim beauty! United we slouch in slack-jawed amazement, craning our heads up, down, left, and right, snapping off as many mental pictures as possible.

Grapevines slither through the limbs like anacondas. The bulging tumor of a high catalpa cracks through its own bark like a swollen brain. Bursts of mistletoe mottle the branches as if stippled by the Great Pointillist.

I still believe in God, I think.

Off in the grainy distance, a glimpse of someone darting from tree to tree. A person, or persons.

"Who was that?" I ask. But the skyline of Carver's secret ghost town distracts him and he hollers.

"Hey, look over here. They's Carter Mill! You kin see the feed mill, the sawmill, the old hotel, the store. And right cheer's the old broke-down barbecue joint!"

Crooked wood-slat buildings slump in defeat, empty as a cicada shell. I shudder to think of the poor suckers who once called this flood zone home. I imagine its glory days being basically what I see now. No progress was ever made, businesses failed, and the only things that grew were the gullies.

True to Carver's word, there is a feed mill, a sawmill, a hotel, a store, and a barbecue shack. CLEM'S MEATS reads the ghost sign above some half-naked cartoon pigs. Like Porky Pig, they wear shirts, but no pants. They're looking back to admire their own butts, as if hungry to eat themselves. But it looks like someone had once painted trousers across their lower halves. Faded brushstrokes hint of a latter attempt at censorship.

"My grand-daddy said that Carter Mill is where the Night Riders usta hide." The Night Riders being a vigilante group of early 20th-century unionized tobacco farmers.

"He said the mayor found out they was all hidin' in the hotel. So he tried to kick 'em out of town. But they bandied together, shot the mayor, and burnt down half the city."

"Did you just see something move out there?" I ask.

"Probably some deer. I been huntin' out here a few times.

Back when I was off the sauce. They's all kinds of turkeys, foxes, rabbits, squirrels, and coyotes too. Painters. Wampus cats. You name it, I've killed it. Damn, I wish I'da brung my gun." Carver stands straddling the bicycle bar looking into the distance, distantly.

"Yep. I was out cheer one day a-huntin' for the White Thang. He's this four-foot-tall albino Wampus cat cain't nobody ketch. I heard him a-singin'. Sounds more like a cryin' little girl. Or a banshee womern a-screamin'. Son, it's effed up. Anyway, every time you see 'im, he's about fitty feet ahead of ya. But whenever you get near, he disappears. But then he'll show up again fitty feet ahead of ya. Hain't no killin' that damn painter."

He means "panther." Carver hocks a loogie and twists his Wranglers, adjusting the fit of his crotch again.

"So anyways. I come across this old boy layin' out here half-dead in the woods... he had't've been huntin' by himself. Well, somebody musta thought he was a deer and shot him. That or the Thang got a holt of 'im. Or maybe he tried to kill himself and missed his brains... or maybe it was all just by happen-chance. Anywho, he was a-layin' there all by hisself, bleedin' out his gullet and tryin' to talk, but only gurgles come out. He looked pretty bad so, um... you know. I had to put 'im down."

"Psssh!"

"No, it's true. I ain't pride of it, but I wouldn't let a *dog* lay there all fell-off like that, would you?"

Carver goes on to describe how he accidentally chipped the man's tooth, shoving in the barrel of the gun. There was a mixture of fear and relief in the man's eyes in that split second before Carver squeezed the trigger. Then... the thunderclap of mercy. A pink explosion of vaporous brains blew out the back of his skull as the sheer force of the gunshot sent the man sitting up for a second. But down he plopped into eternal repose. The poor old boy was off to meet his maker, bless his heart.

Carver lights up a smoke and snaps his Zippo shut to drive the story home.

"Are you kidding me?!" I nervously laugh out loud. "That's the biggest load of crap I've ever heard."

I play along, but I often wonder how far from the truth his legends really stray. Fact is, I haven't known Carver that long, so it could be true, I reckon. I wait for the wink, but this poker-faced murderer affords me no relief. He just looks crazy.

THE DRONE

Carter Mill was founded low in the toxic boglands of a forsaken holler, barren of charm or cheer. Cords of dead vines fray in gestural cross-hatched strokes, like a densely rendered woodcut. The crumbling column of a lone chimney stands like a headstone for a home.

Black birds break the stillness with a rackety bray, and the wind squalls through the timbers with a chilling drone.

"Hear that hum?" Carver asks.

"Yeah, what is that? Seems like it's always humming out here for some reason."

"I got my notions."

It emanates from deep within the woods. Some say it's the sound of cicadas, but everybody knows they sing in the key of C#. After checking on my harmonica, I put this somewhere between B and B♭.

Perhaps The Deadening is seething angst up from the underground. Up through the trees like a pipe organ, or giant lumberhorns, driven by the steams of Hell. I imagine a subterranean network of fibers forming lungs, constricting and expanding like a bellows. Carver tells me that some say it's the sound of pressure being released from a tectonic crack deep beneath the nearby Tennessee River. It issues from vast chasms, as pent-up steam, water, sand, and coal grind, gush, and groan. Come to think of it, I've vaguely heard it all my life around town, coming from the woods in the distance. Wafting across the street to the drugstore.

Rumors of a nearby "Hell Hole" are purported too. They say it's a portal to Earth's core where the chthonian screams of the damned rise to the surface as an immense white noise. I've heard "actual 'Hell Hole' recordings" on late-night AM radio. Some crackpot swore he dropped a microphone down into its depths to capture a more discernible wail of human suffering. Carver believes the droning comes from that secret government facility that puts saltpeter in the water supply ("soft peter," as he calls it). But I prefer to believe it is coming from the haunted harmonium that pumps forever underground.

NOSFERATU

This particular neck o' the woods is where our local "vampire cult" used to meet. They were really just a pathetic gang of teen-age "larpers," role-playing a game they bought at some stupid store at the mall. But, as the world found out, the fun got out of hand.

I'm not sure what exactly they called themselves, but they sure stood out around town. They would mince about in top hats and capes, tapping along the sidewalks with brass-bulbed canes. Some walked with black umbrellas—to protect them from the sun, I reckon. Blood dried in crusty smears around their mouths, and some even had their teeth filed into fangs. Remember, this was all set against the backdrop of a small rural farming community.

So when they weren't hanging out in churchyards, speaking in riddles and killing cats, they were meeting up in a Carter Mill shed to conduct their bloodletting rituals. But, like all things, it got old. So the ringleader—Rod Ferrell, I believe—talked them into taking it up a notch. The plan was to go and kill his girlfriend's parents. He said it would be the ultimate "blood meal." Indeed. T'would be a "grand feast" in which they would all "partake"... and other fancy vampire words.

They met at night in hoodies, hopped in the car, and drove to her folks' place. While the elder couple slept, the kids broke in and bashed their brains in with a clawhammer. I read about it in the paper. It even made it onto *Oprah*. So yeah, it's true.

I remember at the time thinking it was so ridiculous. Vampires? Really? Then again, I suppose small-town kids have to express themselves somehow, especially the creative ones who don't go in for sports. Lord knows I can relate to that.

Plus, these were the days before "social media," so there was no way of accessing a larger goth movement to get a feel for the lifestyle. The limits of the Southern macabre were untested, and suburban latchkey kids were lawless and feral. Come to think of it, "Ferrell" is a fitting name for their leader.

Well, the kids didn't get far. The cops picked them up and they all got life in prison. But copycats kept the movement going for another year. And there were quite a few, actually. They would hang out in public places, making sure everyone saw their pretentious wardrobe and the slice marks on their arms.

Luckily, I only had one run-in with them. One afternoon I went to my favorite coffee shop and was surprised to find it had been redecorated in a gothic manner to cater to the vampires. Most of the lights were dimmed and the interior had been painted black. Some mural-work was supposed to resemble the stone walls of a dungeon, but it just looked like a cheap community theater backdrop. Another crappy small-town misinterpretation of a subculture.

Zit-faced geeks in trench coats lounged on Victorian furniture, reciting bad poetry to one another in fake English accents. A few sat in the back playing chess. It was just so corny I couldn't believe it. I made the error of scoffing aloud, "Are you kidding me? Vampires? Seriously?"

The barista was a fellow I had always joked around with before, but he was not amused this time. He just took my order with his eyes in a dead glaze. Was he one of "them" now, or had his new vampire-friendly training just taken hold? He handed me my coffee and I let myself out amidst a barrage of hissing.

"Whatever," I said back at them. "I hope you all get laid one day."

It was good to be outside. The sun never seemed more refreshing. But as I walked to my car I saw how all four tires had just been slashed.

It is surreal and mildly upsetting to stand in the middle of their old dominion now.

HEADHUNTER

We catch up to a broke down box-truck slumped to the right of the rail bed. The faint sound of calliope music seeps from its bullhorn and warps like a bogged-down tape deck. At first I think it's a lost ice cream truck, but the panels are painted with a sideshow scene. A blond bikini-girl poses in a jungle, unaware of natives approaching through the foliage. You can tell the artist spent more time laboring over her sexy legs and breasts, because they're perfectly rendered. But her slightly cross-eyed face is just an afterthought.

A corn-yellow scroll emblazons above:

SHRUNKEN HEADS OF THE EQUATOR! EACH A
VICTIM OF VOODOO! GODLESS PAGANS, WHY?

"Well, I'll be," says Carver. "How'd this get all the way out cheer?" With a crunch of aluminum, the rear panel heaves open like a motorized garage door. Red velvet curtains are revealed in the doorway, and they hang perfectly still. They are fringed in gold like the edges of a fancy flag. After a few pokes from a pair of mystery hands, the curtains part, and a stocky mustachioed man pops out. He looks like a giant toddler in his shorts and nightgown-length JOURNEY '88 WORLD TOUR t-shirt. The messy red-faced huckster leaps to greet us with nervous energy.

"Steady, fellows. Does the warden know you've escaped?! Ha! I'm just joshing you! What?! Can't ya take a joke? Gentlemen, I apologize. I'm Colonel Joseph T. Strong from Brownsville, Texas."

But before we can even respond...

"Well, gentlemen, it looks like I've taken a wrong turn down the wrong road... which ended up being the wrong shortcut to the wrong damn town altogether! I'm all turned around and my navigational doohickey is on the fritz. Could you two fine sirs tell me how to get to Calvert City?"

"Well, you're not far from Calvert," I reply, "but you are facing the wrong direction."

"Yeah," Carver adds. "If you kin get yer truck pointin' around the other way, you kin hook back out through the trailhead. I just ripped down the chain, so you orta be able to go up and hang a right."

"Much obliged for the directions, but I'm afraid this brings us to my next dilemma. As you can see, my mighty galleon has run ashore. She's fine on pavement but these old gravel roads are a terror, even though she's been coast-to-coast twelve times! But you two look young and healthy enough to lend a hand. Would you mind setting me back on solid ground? Would you mind giving me a push?"

"Only if you let us take a gander at whatcha got in the back there." Carver nods up with his chin.

"Want a free tour, do ya? Well, I'll be happy to show you! You will soon feast your eyes on the terrible fleshen trophies of the heathen tribes of Peru. As you can see from the pulchritudinous panel of my truckside tableau, each severed head is a tragic testament to the perils of paganism! Each one, a witness for Christ!

Gentlemen, make haste, heave ho, and the free tour is yours for the taking!"

Leaning in, I whisper to Carver, "This has got to be the coolest-slash-weirdest thing I've ever run into."

We push Colonel Strong's truck around while he stands on the running board, half in the cab and half out, steering with his right hand and holding the door open with his left, hollering, "Mush! Mush!" the whole time.

"Steady, fellows. Steady as she goes!" With one last heave, the truck is set right and it's time for our free tour.

Colonel Strong steps down from the cab, widens his eyes, tiptoes slowly to the back, and motions with his index finger. It lures us in like the wormtongue of a snapping turtle.

He leaps upon the rusty back bumper to begin his routine, surprisingly graceful for such a compact little slob.

"Excellent, gentlemen. Excellent. Now for your reward. Who shall be first?"

Carver seems particularly fired up, so I wave him on with a smile. Up the steps and soon to pierce the darkness. He turns to look back at me but the drapes swallow him like plasma.

It seems an eternity. I've been left here for some time now, with just the white whisper of the leaves and the humming woodnotes of the forest to keep me company. That and the sagging tape of calliope songs. I might be wrong, but it sounds like there's something else playing beneath the chewed-up circus music. The sound of a crying woman being interrogated, slapped around. The faint impression of a man punching and yelling. It fades in and out beneath the strains of "Waltzing Matilda."

Carver exits the curtain at last, rubbing his neck and half-smiling out of politeness.

"Next!" kids the pitchman. "Whoa, whoa, whoa! Not all at once, ladies and gentlemen! Form an orderly queue in a single file!"

"What'd ya think?" I ask.

"Pretty cool." Carver pauses. "I reckon them South Americans didn't keer much fer you palefaces neither. Or fer one another, fer that matter. Go have a looksee, I reckon."

Colonel Strong extends a hand and all at once I am gathered into his realm of mystery. After 30 seconds of utter darkness waiting for the Colonel to find the dimmer switch, the orange wire of a decorative candle-bulb awakens a display of death.

Thousands of prune-like shrunken heads hang like dried delicacies in an Asian market. I count a dozen to a cord, clustered like strands of garlic. But this ain't produce. These are people! You can see each of their tiny, horrible faces, like taut zip-lipped little scrotums, displayed so densely that there is literally nowhere to stand without having them touch you.

Colonel Strong pushes through to the back, heads bobbing in his wake like wind chimes. I follow behind, tucked in a ball, squinting and wincing and spitting tiny hairs from my face. The soft bouncing weight of each leathery cluster sends shivers down my spine.

He stops at the rear of the room where rows of "pickled punks" are set up on a table. Dozens of jarred human fetuses suspend in amber repose. A plankton of flesh floats around the stillborn specimens, their mongoloid eyes awash in urine-colored poison.

"Planned Parenthood!" he cries. "Where the fetal meets the fatal! Heathen cannibals of modern times! The cruel tradition continues today!"

"You probably work a lot of churches and revivals, don't you?"

"Indeed I do, sir. Indeed I do."

"Ever heard of the Reverend Tazewell?"

"Ever heard of him? Why, I knew him like a brother! We used to work the same dope show back in the 1970s. Before we both found the LORD, that is. It was in 1993 when I heard the WORD for the first time. But I remember like it was yesterday! It was a South Carolina puppet show. Excuse me, a puppet ministry! And when that fuzzy little muppet told us about how Procter & Gamble gives 100 percent of its profits to the Church of Satan, well, my friend, I walked that aisle lickety-split. I went up and kneeled before that little cardboard castle. And I grabbed that little fella, tears streaming down my face, and begged him to show me the way. Been on the straight and narrow ever since!"

I explain my connection to Tazewell while admiring some antique maps tacked to a corkboard. The tea-colored charts are marked with little foil stars that indicate the places where head-hunting was practiced (and perhaps still is).

I turn to exit, preparing myself for the sensation of weaving back through a bunch of withered little pouch-heads. And with a deep breath, I duck and aim for the skinny sliver of light between the red curtains. And even though I feel a slight pinch, I am finally free… reunited with Carver and standing outside on the Old Spur Line.

After a few more words of pretension, the Colonel bids us "adieu" and we wave good-bye. As he peels out, I imagine the G-force swinging his tiny passengers in back. Gravel goes flying and his exhaust cloud looks like a fresh ghost released into writhing oblivion.

It takes a few minutes for the smoke to settle, but at last it is clear. Clear enough for Carver and me to compare the strange baby-sized bite marks on our necks.

Chapter Five
SIN EATER

He inches along like a wretched Rumpelstiltskin. The little jesus-creature in the corner of my eye. In the corner of my mind.

He is summoned to his terrible duties, rising up from the floorboards of a woesome woodshed. He greets the dawn with a black-tongued hiss. Morning mist glazes his naked structure. It soaks into the mash of his unnatural makings: a meat-and-lumber frame held together with chicken wire, twine, skin, and nails.

He is a re-animated ground-crawler. A stickman. A golem. A scourge. A haint. A pariah of the gullies. And this land is his home.

Fog banks hang in the river bottoms like idling white ironclads. Yonderways, our little critter ambles through the fading moonlight and slides into the swamp. It's an indecent time of day for anything to move about, and he knows that full well. Yeah, the hours suck. But, hey, it's a job.

His legs are like the bamboo walking sticks of an Alabama Dixiecrat. Skinny and ringed, knobby and bowed. His armbones bend at obscene angles, like a carpenter's folding ruler. They are sleeved in the tattoo ink of Scripture, the Book of Leviticus, specifically. The full text is scrimshawed there in a scroll of misspelled chicken-scratch. And the writing contrasts harshly with his pearly-white flesh.

He is an expressionistic Christ-form from a medieval reliquary. An apostate leper, whose lungs wheeze with lost air. But no oxygen escapes the gills along his gullet. He slides effortlessly through the ooze of un-drained malarial morasses. He burrows into the earthen lair of catfish canals. The sunlight that streams through crawdad holes illuminates his passage underground. He is utterly suited to this realm, as tight as a ball joint is suited to its socket. He puts the "man" in "salamander."

The stenches of stagnant ditches, which you or I find repulsive, are his manner of navigation. Each stinking hint of rot and ruin contains the subtleties that guide him on like starlight. Snaking through root systems, he emerges from the portholes of tree knots. An ancient villain of abstract purpose.

Then up he hooks his ten-penny fingernails into the bark, climbing like a sloth into the canopy. He is sluggish yet sly, hungry and hellbent. And he is the "What-Is-It" that has called me here today. The homunculus heart of the forest.

Chapter Six
A CONFUSION OF FOWL

Surprises found in Carter Mill.

WERIFESTERIA

Sometimes, in places this bleak, I have to force myself to take a breath, think of better times, and concentrate on happy thoughts. That's when my mind floods with visions of long-ago summer vacations. Rolling hills of bluegrass welcomed my young eyes to a budding appreciation of nature. I recall lying in the tall grass of a valley to watch golden clouds zeppelin by. All by myself, I'd sit and craft little boats from lumber scraps, poke for crawdads with grass stalks, shoot my slingshot, and splash into the creek from a swinging vine. The weather was warm and balmy, and each Maxfield Parrish sunset proved more than my young heart could take. More than my old soul can now bear to remember.

I dream of that shadowy creek, with all its knotty roots and moss, iron ore, clay beds, and whispering currents. It was God's own water garden, and I had just happened upon it one day. A complete accident. Just one county over from here.

Deep blue-greens cooled the lush Elysium. Flat rocks and toadstools perhaps hid the homes of gnomes and elves. Even

Pan Himself could have appeared before me commanding worship, as in *The Wind in the Willows*, and I would have obliged. It was all too glorious not to honor in earnest.

But, once I left, I was never able to retrace my steps. No matter the trail, I had lost it forever. Maybe it had been a dream, or my mind had become cluttered with so many comic books that I'd lost the mojo to find it. It's one of the great tragedies of my life.

This forest city, Carter Mill, stands in sharp contrast to that Shangri-La. Grays replace greens, browns replace blues. But, unlike most folks, I can appreciate the so-called "off colors," the ones not found in a box of Crayolas. Now that I'm grown, I marvel at all of Nature's many forms of intensity. And, ever since Daddy died, I've even developed a taste for the aesthetics of death.

Or haven't you noticed?

THE LOBED MOUNTAIN CHILD

Before we saddle up, Carver and I stop to take a leak. Through the branches of my bathroom, I can see the banks of Clarks River. They are blanketed with yet more thick green Kudzu. Their leaves hang like pennants: leathery, languid, and full of ticks. Blackjack vines lace through the treetops like circus wires. Woolly mammoths and brontosauruses parade in gray-green shapes. The Devil's Topiary.

Kudzu, AKA *Pueraria montana-lobata*, is of Chinese descent, and as such, has good reason to want to do us in—Communist plot that it must be. Deceptively, it begins as just a tiny thing. Its little runners spread via "vegetative reproduction," producing shoots that root along its host. The seeds it sheds in autumn lie dormant for years, long after the pest has been thought destroyed. Yet, once again, it stirs, deep below our boots, in the loam and gloam of the shadowlands.

And although deaf and blind, it maneuvers around the urns of sleeping saints, through the soil of the biblical Sheol. Here the earth is churned by the weed's slow sinew. Like a constrictor, it girdles the good roots around it. Then up it slips, piercing the topsoil into daylight. It climbs to the treetops to unfurl its shroud of dragon scales, and kills the trees with shade.

Fig. 2
Kudzu
(Pueraria
Lobata)

Oaks, pines, walnuts, sycamores. They are the good guys. They stand as strong as they can against their Kudzu cousin, digging their feet in to do battle. Because, as you may know, the roots of trees often run deeper than the branches grow wide.

It's true. If we could view a cross-section of Earth's crust, we'd see how the woods above cannot compare to the wilderness growing underground. Believe it or not, this vast, gripping web is what footholds us to the planet. It reinforces our topsoil and gives humans a place to stand. Killer Kudzu, however, seems hell-bent on loosening these underpinnings, weakening our purchase, and sending us all flying into outer space.

THE LAST SUPPER

Interestingly enough, Kudzu is edible. Folks down here have been known to cook it into a "sallet" (or salad), boil it like collard greens, and douse it with Tabasco to help it go down. But, let's be honest. Kudzu is more likely to eat you.

We're really not that different from plants. Consider the fractal makeup of the human body. Observe how each of our extremities branch into smaller and smaller parts. Arms and legs grow out from a trunk. Hands and feet grow out from arms and legs. Fingers and toes grow out from hands and feet. So are we that much superior to Kudzu, a plant with infinite extremities?! A plant that triumphs over tall-columned verandas and mighty castle spires? Over entire empires?

For not long after the footprints of man have faded into dust will Kudzu and all the other green things of the world join forces to stake back their claim. Like mold overtaking a corpse.

After all, it was their fruit in the Garden that first tricked us. Now they wait, biding their time for our sins to find us. Waiting for the day when our last city is toppled and they can finally pounce. They will release their runners to go sailing through our ruins and into our bodies, spanning the globe round and round to bind the planet into one giant Irish knot.

But let's be a good sport about it. Let us bring forth, once again, the forbidden fruit of Eden. Wring its red nectar down in succulent currents. Replenish to the brim the very Holy Grail of Christ and have a toast!

Remarkable old wizards! Warped, twisting elders! In the end, they will kick our butts.

So to the victor the spoils!

THE APPROACH

The tinkling of chain links and the clonk of a cowbell pierce the air. We scan the skyline for cattle. Nothing.

"Let's check it out," whispers Carver. "It come from the sawmill."

After kickstanding our bikes, we slide down a ridge of crushed stone into the stagnation of Clarks River. The black liquid barely ripples against our boots as we wade deeper into the muck. The phlegm of frog spawn circles stalks of cattails. The girth of cypress trunks settle near the water's edge, billowing at the base as if liquid bark has been poured down a pole to harden. It slowly flows on like batter, channeling off from itself again and again like antlers, only to harden into the knuckles that grip the time-clawed clay.

Dragonflies descend. Telephone bugs, bumblebees, and dirt daubers. All of Nature is protesting our arrival. We swat them away and escape through a curtain of wisteria. It hangs like the camo of an army camp.

Once to the other side, we clodhop to a hill of sandstone where the scratch of a path leads farther into the woods.

Along the way, I notice a rusty horseshoe hanging lucky-side-down in the fork of a redbud. With a solid tug, I find it is sunk in deep, grown over by the bark and solid as a wand of rebar protruding from concrete. It's as if the redbud has found a human-made trinket to flaunt and prove that flora, like fauna, are no dumb creatures.

CLANG!

The ghastly chime rings out again.

"It's comin' from around back." Carver points with a head tilt.

O the tintinnabulation of Hell! I'm giddy with ghoulish anticipation. My imagination runs wild. Could it be a mad blacksmith in a flickering cave? The devil's hammer in a fire-lit pit?

ARCHAEOPTERYX

After scuttling alongside the rotting planks of a millwheel, we round the corner like pretend spies, past a scrapyard of failed industry. A redneck dump of old, rusty washing machines and iceboxes spill down the creekbank at random angles of mid-topple, each one looking like a freeze-frame of failure. In fact, they're mired so deep in the muck, it's as if they've been there forever—revealed only now by some archeological dig. Farm implements sit fixed in a stove of corrosion. The copper ball of an old moonshine-still lies splayed by a revenuer's axe. It's like a murder weapon buried in a potbelly. The ball is just a blown-out bucket now, collecting filthy tar-colored sump. It stinks to high heaven and everything around us is seized-up and foul.

Out of the vagueness, the shape of a struggling bird emerges. A vulture roosts atop a farrier's stovepipe chimney. It is slump-ing under the burden of a collar and bell.

"Well I'll be double-dipped," Carver shout-whispers. "It's that Bell'd Buzzard! I hain't seen him in years! My brother's the one what slapped that thang on 'im. Years ago. This bird is famous!"

Ah yes, Carver's brother. Skitch Canute. The only person I know who is crazier than Carver. That redneck's gone and gar-roted a buzzard with a dog collar and a cowbell.

Understand, Skitch Canute is the type of hillbilly who bur-ies his money in canning jars and has a concealed carry permit to protect himself against a "zombie uprising." He believes the Freemasons "run the show" and refuses to pay taxes. And he brags that he once beat a blind man to death with his own cane. Some Mexican over in Graves County, I believe. "Smart mouth had it comin'."

The buzzard shifts its weight from foot to foot, fanning the sun in a strobe of feathers. And then… its caw: *Craghhhh*. A startling melody of pain.

"Yeah, Skitch stuck that bell on him, that old jasper. He caught it and trained it to do tricks. He learnt it how to shake hands and take a bow. Then he heard that if you split their tongues in two you kin learn 'em how to talk. But it didn't work. The bird just kept tryin' to escape. Skitch stuck that bell on it so we could track it down.

"But it finally got away and people started talkin' about it. At least the ones in Skitch's trailer park. So he thought it'd be interestin' if it just became a legend. I'm the one who made up the name Bell'd Buzzard."

The old vulture lurches on the chimney, tending its sores and lolling its forked tongue. It is struggling against the collar with a time-hardened nervous tick. Poor thing. Visually, it is a throwback to the fearsome Archaeopteryx. Mange forms scales around its elbowed throat and molted beak, and it looks like some birdshot pellets have peppered it too. What a sad sight! But, relatively speaking, buzzards are fairly new around here, to this line of latitude. So you almost can't blame the local yokels for picking on them. That's just what they do. Hell, they don't know any better. Hillbillies are part of the animal kingdom too.

Peering into the senile eyes of this cryptic specimen, I imagine it to be the lost "Crow-a-Tone" of the Roanoke colony, or perhaps some reincarnated small-town crier ringing his alarm. Resembling only the dregs of the lowliest caste, its jagged feathers splay like the broken fingers of a begging slave. It's a heartbreaking thing to behold. Harbinger of doom. Scavenger of ruin. If I had the guts, I'd put the damn thing down myself.

"It'll be fine," Carver says, sensing my pity. "It's lasted this long. And that's fresh blood on its wing. It's eatin' well."

With our mystery solved, we say goodbye to the Bell'd Buzzard and slop our way back through the reek.

Bullfrogs bellow in the creek like the reeds of a baritone woodwind. I heard once that stagnant water can change a frog into a turtle, or a moth into an owl, or a horsehair into a snake. Luckily the stench is getting fainter as we approach our bikes.

I step on a branch that cracks a warning signal to a chattering field of starlings. *Whoosh!*

A real sonic boom erupts as a million wings take flight. The force is incredible. We can feel it in our chests! Like a breath of thalassic power blown from the lips of the North Wind, the gust knocks us back and topples the barbecue shack to the ground.

The birdcloud curls off into the sky like smoke. Miles of little souls bearing away news of our arrival.

PERSPECTIVE

We sally our bikes past the outskirts of Carter Mill, over to where the rail bed takes form again. Twin walls of divided forest flank our trail and diminish to the rippling ridge of the horizon.

They remind me of the walls of the parted Red Sea, making Carver and me the children of Israel. Blink twice and now they are the high decks of two armadas in standoff. A breeze makes their masts sway as if truly upon the water. Crows' nests drape with an ivy of netting.

But this retreating perspective may also be viewed as an encroaching presence. Perhaps it is an embrace. Or maybe it's the spread legs and seducing inner thighs of Nature, drawing us ever deeper into her bewitching vulval bloom.

Over yonder, the mast of a bladeless windmill casts its shadow upon yet another outmoded farm implement that has rusted to a halt... and Eli Whitney weeps in Heaven. Somewhere out of sight a dog barks and a horse nays.

"I once had a crippled dog named Arithmetic. When he ran he 'put down three and carried the one.'"

Now Carver is thinking of one.

"Well, I had a dog with brass balls and no hind legs. We called 'im Sparky!"

Chapter Seven
THE UNBLINKING EYE

In defense of the "Southern Fantasy Novel."
A Southern bestiary.
The South today.

Let me pause to ask a question. Is this story too far-fetched? Too "out there"? Well, then. I will remind the reader...

Venturing into the wilderness in search of reward is a theme as old as the hills. My reward will be the bragging rights of having found the Kudzu House and the vanquishing of my foe, Stoney Kingston, the liar and thief of my One True Love. It's something I just need to prove to myself. Or, as George Leigh Mallory said, I just need to go "because it is there."

Other precedents exist also. The humanities have long lauded the likes of such noble heroics. Like the deeds of Beowulf, Odysseus, Hercules, Merlin, Galahad, and Ivanhoe. Yes, I'll grant you, their legends are set against far more voluptuous lands than this American South. They are based in antiquity or medieval Europe, surrounded by mystic mountains, forlorn fjords, and the sunless vaults of half-year darkness. Corpse-cold bastions and palaces of plenty. Teutonic old castles and thatched-roof cottages. Dark forests and bogs overrun with hobgoblins, gnomes, and ogres. Yes, I know, I know.

But should it confound us to hear that our modern American South provides a similar spectral backdrop? Or will the reader deem my Southern Iliad and Odyssey an "Idiocy and Oddity"?

Have millions of acres of protected Southern forests, swamps, and mountains escaped our attention? Or have we forgotten about our own hidden villains? What about our own Grendel, "Big Foot," and his hirsute kin? There's the Skunk Ape of Florida, the Fouke Monster of Arkansas, and the Hoofenogger of Tennessee, just to name a few.

Don't believe me?

EXHIBIT A.

It is written, by our own American scribes, reports of Southern "giants" in a county not far from here:

> Among the passengers the other night bound for New York from Kentucky on the day express was a wild man, who occupied a seat in smoking car No. 158. He was accompanied by James Harvey and Raymond Boyd [who] were on their way to Bridgeport, Conn., to make arrangements with P.T. Barnum to exhibit their prize in conjunction with his circus. [The wild man's] hair reaches nearly to his waist and falls over his shoulders, completely covering his back; his beard is long and thick, while his eyebrows are much heavier than those of an ordinary human being.
>
> Boyd and Harvey [had] built a man-trap for him [...] and placed a big piece of beef in it. They watched the trap for three days.

In his cave, [they] found the skeletons of small
animals and skins of over fifty of the most
venomous snakes.

—"A Kentucky Wild Man,"
Newark Advocate, 1883.

But there are even more Southern monsters! Dare we ignore
Johnny Creek of Maxon Mill, the Goatman of Pope Lick
Creek, Fishhead of Reelfoot Lake, or the Gray Man of Pawleys
Island? Their horrific faces have hissed at neither Anglo nor
Saxon, Goth nor Visigoth. Nay, nary a Norman, in the shadow
of Eilean Donan, has slain La Chupacabra. And never has an
AIDS Wolf darkened the door of the old German Heidelberg.

But ask any old hillbilly and you'll get an earful. For these
creatures, and the baleful lands they stalk, are strictly American,
and Southern for the most part. They are as much a part of us
as our penchant for fried chicken and turnip greens.

LEVIATHAN

And what of the great water serpents? Of course we are all
familiar with the blessed text from whence all saints draw fear:

[...] with his sore and great and strong sword
shall [He] punish leviathan the piercing serpent, even leviathan that crooked serpent; and
He shall slay the dragon that is in the sea.

—Isaiah 27:1 KJV

However, to my knowledge the LORD has yet to return for
this epic final fishing trip. It has always been up to us, and the
mortal likes of Nemo, Ahab, and Cousteau.

Their tales recount many a serpent of the Seven Seas. But
is it unimaginable that these great gilled beasts might have

adapted to the brackish inlets and fresh waterways of America? How quickly we forget our elementary school lessons! What of Hiawatha's giant sturgeon? Or the alligator gar found in Lake Barkley? Is it such a leap that Kentucky, with the world's densest congestion of navigable rivers (and more coastline than Florida!) could hide the lumbering coils of such monsters?

To be sure, it is indeed within the realm of Southern possibility! For here is…

EXHIBIT B., written by the Southern hand of experience:

> A huge, strange reptile is reported from the Pond River bottoms of this county, many persons declaring to have seen it. Its presence is causing great alarm […]
>
> One man who described his experience with the monster, says he was driving a team of mules hitched to a wagon along the route which led through woods when he heard a great crashing in the underbrush and the great snake raced into the roadway onto the wagon. The snake, he says, became entangled in the front wheels of the vehicle and lifted its head above the dashboard with its huge mouth wide open. The driver says he leaped to the ground and ran, abandoning his mules and wagon.
>
> Glancing back over his shoulder he says he saw the snake overturn the wagon, whereupon the mules ran away, demolishing the wagon.
>
> —"Kentucky Section Is Terrorized
> by An Immense Snake,"
> *Mitchell Evening Republican,* June 2, 1925.

There is no shortage of wild snakes, wild men, big cats, and goblins in our protected Kentucky reserves. What we lack, however, are likeminded warriors to go hunt them down. It seems as if folklorists, the ones who make it their business to collect these stories, are too busy sitting in their studies, composing longwinded essays on the nuances of Southern mythology. Apparently, they are content to just sit there and collect their knowledge secondhand. But where's the fun in that?

Yes, as adventurers, Carver and I are out to meet these monsters face to face. But we are on our own. You would think the boredom that comes with modern convenience would motivate a new warrior class: an Adventure Team dead set on doing battle with dragons. Call it some sort of backlash of bravado, or a war on post-modern apathy and leisure. Sadly, no. It's a different breed coming up these days.

THE RURAL PURGE

As to the demographics of men in the the "New South" and how it relates to heroism… well, the times, they have changed. Indeed, in 1927, American agrarianism commenced its official decline. The majority of Americans began making their living by becoming employed by The System. As a result, the old homestead ways of life have ceased. That era has all but slid down the collective memory hole like so much slop down a sluice. Along with it, many a manly conquest has followed suit, replaced with virtual adventure, overstuffed furniture, air-conditioning, and TV dinners. Trite but true: technology has ostensibly solved most of our problems yet created entirely new ones to take their place.

At the time of this writing, our most recent great advance has been the marrying of the party line to the television screen and an adjoining typewriter. Read: the "Personal Computer," the "Internet," and its corresponding "Information Age."

Unfortunate side effects include narcissism, the mass delusion of self-celebrity, and a willful surrender of privacy. With the collective knowledge of the universe at their fingertips, most prefer flashy manufactured news items and pornography. Shiftless magpie mankind has been outed to be! However, biologically speaking, the new men of the South are still the same as ever. I mean, they still have a tall, strong frame, but it's solely the result of their genetic Y chromosome. Their Southern drawl is weakening with each passing year and their voices are getting softer. There are, after all, fewer cattle to call in and zero words of discipline allowed by society to be raised toward their children. So gone forever are the hard-hewn vocal rumbles, whistles, and hoarse overtones that evoke subconscious respect.

And the worst enemy the post-agrarian male must face? His own body. Sad to say, the prime directive of his wiring is to store fat for survival. No longer required to work the fields in this reconstructed New South, the poor bastard is doomed just to sit there gaining weight like a blob in suburbia—plopped down like a wet column of dog food, stuck in the shape of the can.

And there he'll forever sit, beneath the pilgrim-hat-shaped roof of his tacky McMansion, steadily growing into his upholstery. (Hence the Southern obesity epidemic.)

The resulting bedsores of the laziest ones have literally healed into the fabric of their couches and a new hybrid of monster is born.

EXHIBIT C.

A 480-pound Martin County resident has died after emergency workers tried to remove the person's rear end from a couch where it had remained for about six years.

The 40-year-old died Wednesday after a failed

six-hour effort to dislodge their backside from the couch. Workers say the home was filthy, and the person had been too large to get up to even use the bathroom.

Everyone going inside the home had to wear protective gear. The stench was so powerful they had to blast in fresh air. A preliminary autopsy on the body lists the cause of death as "morbid obesity." The person died at Martin Memorial Hospital South, still attached to the couch.

—"480-Pound Shut-In Dies
After Six Years On Couch,"
Channel 9 WFTV, Florida.

But these half-human/half-couch creatures that dwell in squalor are of no interest to Carver and me. Neither is the evil blue flicker of the "Unblinking Eye" that televises their marching orders to just sit there and consume.

Don't get me wrong, I still believe in the South. For festering deep inside these temperpaedic bubbas was, and still is, a latent vanquisher. Is it so hard to believe that at least two of them, Carver and myself, have actually escaped their furniture to discover this within themselves?

We have resisted the lure of the Sauron-like "CBS" Eye and other TV devils that would have us stay put. Now we seek out actual devils (what the Southern Pentecostals call "haints"). We delve farther and farther down the Old Spur Line, as its worming gullet swallows us whole, consuming us with concentric rows of rail-spike teeth. Still we spiral deeper and deeper into the yawning maw, giddy for what nightmares await!

Ghosts and serpents. Wild men and wolves. Quicksand and landslides. Hookmen, goat-suckers, and giant spider webs. You can't look me in the eye and tell me these things don't exist down here.

> *The "Warlord of all Bloodshed"*
> *Is under the floorboard of the woodshed.*

Yes, if ever the Devil was incarnate on earth, it is down South right now… hiding in the Kudzu. And I've got a machete!

Chapter Eight
THE STUBBLEFIELDS

The barrens.
A graveyard discovered.
"Melungeons."

"Careful not to put yer eye out. It's all run scald up cheer. Land's got teeth."

I survey the ground where the Old Spur Line fades into a landscape of hardscrabble. Snapped corn stalks and fallen branches spike up out of the dirt like tusks. It's the debris field of the long-gone Rosebank Plantation. Once lush with tobacco, now its dead, dry furrows crease Earth's worried brow.

"The Davis Twins both lost an eye horsin' around out cheer in the Stubblefields," Carver warns. "All these widow-makers and roots sticking up outta the mud kin trip ya up. If you accidentally fall, they kin pop yer eyeballs clean outcher skull."

"Davis Twins? Are those the same guys who started the Shotgun Wars back in the '90s? We usta could hear them shootin' at one another from my house."

"Yeah. Hell, we'd all hide out and shoot at the Davis Twins. I got peppered a few times but it ain't nothin' unless they're a-shootin' point blank. But when they started havin' them

swordfights I said no-thank-you. Hell, Buck Davis had one o'
his nipples chopped off with a hatchet!"

"So now he's got one eye and one nipple?"

"Ha! Yeah, I reckon so!" Carver hoots.

"Left eye. Right nipple!"

PLACE MEMORY

Here lies an ugly plat with a tragic antebellum past. Chimney
stacks and Greek columns mark where the plantation once
stood. Slave quarters survive in back, dangling with old chains.
Chains that rattle when the wind is still. And in the shadows,
ghosts in gray uniforms repeat the last minutes of their lives in
an eternal loop. Civil War re-enactors of a different kind.

In every nook and cranny, in any direction on God's green
earth, there is history to be learned. In fact, it doesn't matter
if it's a shimmering sea of parked cars or the most suburban
of front yards. There is a fascinating historical story unique to
those coordinates. Never mind that all of this, everything, was
once molten matter spiraling through space. That alone blows
my mind. But imagine anywhere in the world, modern or mundane. It doesn't matter. It was once home to something special.
Perhaps there was a rare race of giant crocodile that crawled
around there back in Paleolithic times. Or maybe Vikings plod-
ded through the mud when Lewis and Clark were but twinkles
in their daddies' eyes. Imagine all those Thunderbolt Cherokee
patting their mud-yurt villages into shape eons before the Trail
of Tears led them to Hell. Man, I don't know. A small-town kid
has to cook up something interesting about his own backyard.
Collecting folktales and courting ghosts is just another way for
the rural-lonely to stay sane.

Expert of experts, Carver Canute informs me we are actually
in the land of...

THE MELUNGEONS

"This usta be where the Melungeons come to make whiskey. They hid over in that ditch. When the coast was clear they come out and turned this whole area into their squat.

"They was mountain gypsies," he adds. "They're black, but they're not black black. Nobody knows really what they are. They're just gypsies, hillbilly gypsies. Abe Lincoln was half Melungeon!"

"No way."

Melungeon is a hillbilly malapropism for the word *mulatto*. It is believed they are the descendants of the Turk and Portuguese immigrants that went missing from the lost colony of Roanoke. They eventually settled in deep Appalachia.

"Yep, he got it on his mama's side. They's a Melungeon grave-yard up ahead. I'll prove it to ya."

It's an obstacle course of cornstalks, roots, gopher trails, and wood, and it is starting to get old. We're constantly having to walk around something. It takes all the brainpower I can muster to navigate my bike through the chunky maze, this *terra dentata*. A bunch of woodpiles form an archipelago across the field. Lumber piles… stick piles. To me, they look like pyres awaiting their witches.

We hobble some five acres more to a crisp, verdant grove of pine and cedar, the trees, according to Carver, that demand the most respect.

"Granny said the LORD likes the pines best of all His trees. Cedars especially. They take a long time to grow, their wood is true, and it's in the Bible."

Or "bobble," as he pronounces it.

"King James."

"I would've figured your granny worshipped the Great Spirit, or something more… Cherokee."

"Well, she thought it was all the same thing. Just called differ-ent names. They's actually a buncha Indian gods, but the White

Man wanted us to just hold to the One. They's the cemetery, see the sign?"

Framed in white wrought iron, the message reads:

ST. JUDE'S GARDEN
COME BLOOMING YOUTHS AS YOU PASS BY,
AND ON THESE LINES DO CAST AN EYE.
AS YOU ARE, SO ONCE WAS I;
AS I AM NOW, SO MUST YOU BE;
PREPARE FOR DEATH AND FOLLOW ME.

We descend into the shady dank of St. Jude's Garden. It is a moist, echoing grotto from another time. A Stonehenge of mausoleums. Each footstep meets a cold cobblestone that floats in a billiard carpet of moss. This path leads us inside a ten-foot-tall inner ring of looming tombs, and I find myself dreaming of the restfulness that could be had here. O to find my own little plot! That special hole in the ground that sighs for me. Coffinwood cradling like a bassinette. Such enveloping comfort, I scarcely can wait!

The occasional kicked pebble ricochets off the granite as our strange procession leads us out to the rest of the graveyard. Bowing pinetops close in around us, bathing us in gray. Another crumbling mausoleum stands ahead, accompanied by obelisks and more cooling cedars.

What a find! admires my inner archeologist. The crypt comes complete with gargoyles, medieval traceries, and little glass vignettes. The vignettes are cameo-shaped portraits preserved behind a lens of lacquer. Like little lockets of trapped souls, each disc faces sunrise awaiting Christ, marking the catacomb of one God's-honest Melungeon.

"They're real!" I squint to admire them one at a time.

Stern, swarthy faces stare back from behind a haze of varnish. Crickets chirp between the stepping-stones.

"That's what they look like?"

"They're like old Eye-talians fresh off the boat on Elvis Island," Carver answers. "They buried 'em out here 'cause they's Catholic. Back then they usta think the priests were devils. My Grampa Zeb said he once seed a priest without his beanie on. He said he seen his devil horns.

"Check this out." Carver picks up a lump of cement about the size and shape of a softball.

"What is it?"

"It's a grape. Look up yonder."

Craning my head back, I see the outstretched wings of a concrete angel atop a forty-foot pedestal. She stands tall, wielding a terrible, slow sword and dangling a seductive cluster of grapes above the earth. Rebar sprigs out from the bunch like realistic stems.

"When the final grape drops, it'll be Judgment Day."

"What are you going to do with that one?"

"I'm gonna keep it." He shoves it in his pocket and disappears around the bend.

I take another parting glance at the eroding grapes of wrath and count a remaining... three.

"Holy crap. The end is nigh!"

Carver pops his head from around a gravestone to *pssst* me over to the corner of another mausoleum.

"Look," he whispers. "You kin see their bones."

I walk over and peer down into a washed-away corner. Through marble and dirt I can make out the calcium remnants of a Melungeon body. A section of skull sits half-buried in a hole of powdery silt.

"How'd you find this place?" I ask.

"Skitch used t'come out here on his dirt bike looking for Big Foot. He'd pop whip-its off the fresh graves around back."

Carver stares silently for a second and continues: "Skitch is an asshole."

"Yeah."

"When we were kids, he locked me in the clothes dryer and left it on fer a whole ire. I had to go to the hospital fer first- and second-degree burns."

"What can I say?"

"We done said it. Skitch is an asshole."

All around the outside of the tomb are the flattened head-stones of an even lowlier class. Melungeon soldiers, forgotten by their country. The gardens cease to bloom along this lonely row where the leaves won't lie. No wind. No rain. Even Nature herself didn't bother to water their weeds every Decoration Day. Sadly, the only things that grow here are the gray hairs and fingernails of the coffined dead.

The shadows of branches rake across the epitaphs.

EARLY ANTONIO FUGATE JR.
USA
"LIKE SOLDIERS IN THE FIELD,
DRUMMERBOYS MUST ALSO DIE"
1851-1864

HYMAN CORNETT
USA
"BLOODY FIELDS BLOSSOM BLUE IN TIME"
1833-1864

ELECTRICITY X
DEAR SON
USA
"MAMA WAS A DYNA.
DADDY WAS A MOE.
EVERY DYNAMO MAKES
ELECTRICITY."
1850-1865

It's obvious that many of these poor "colored folks" were conscripted Union soldiers sent to the frontlines. Carver says that as non-Africans they were born free men, but they were isolated and poor. But it was a time when poverty was at least noble, and even commoners had a higher purpose. You wouldn't know it from these unkempt graves though. Lost to time, they are unfit for tribute. The wind whistles a belated requiem as my mind wanders:

Is there really no God? No Heaven? Is it really all for nothing? Are we not owed an explanation of some sort? If so, what a waste! I really hope there's a God. And not an all-knowing One, because then I'd be angry at Him for all the evil and suffering. Yeah, I hope He's kind of a dumbass. With coke-bottle glasses, mismatched socks, and maybe his fly is open. Because how can you stay mad at that?

Chapter Nine
SIN EATER Part 2

He hears The Call inside the void where his heart would be. For within his chest cavity swings a canvas pouch upon a brass cuphook, screwed into the timber of his ribcage. It brims over with the iniquities of the townspeople, leaving trails that run down like coffee stains. His gut rattles with the trinkets and toys swiped from the bedsides of sick children. But he is a thief of more than just whatnots and doodads. He drools with an insatiable appetite for disease, death, and destruction.

Unfortunately, these horrible features are wholly hidden to the outside world. That's because he is a shape-shifter too. Were he to walk about town, you'd just see a homeless human charity-case with a harelip and a lazy eye. You'd see another poor old middle-aged soul, afflicted with acute inbreeding, Asperger's, or some other snag of fate. That's his disguise! But his sad face, drooping posture, and thrift store wardrobe can't hide the truth. He may go about his day with his little Elmer Fudd cap pulled down low, fitting in as best he can. But he doesn't fool me!

I truly believe him to be a "Sin Eater" who, like Christ, is a devourer of man's evils. He takes on our transgressions so that we might be cleansed. Anyone can see that! But you choose not to.

Why, just look at his gin blossoms. Weren't those once the blemishes of our late town drunk, Nub Prather? And those venereal sores around his mouth? Why, he got those off that Ruby Walters floozy. But come on! Think about it! Ask yourself how that's possible! She's been dead some sixty-odd years now!

Chapter Ten
SOUTH ELECTRIC EYES (S.E.E.)

A secret code unlocked.
The Realm of the Red Snake.
Gunplay.

Farther on, a row of tender Little Lamb statues marks the graves of babies. Vandals like Skitch, or winter ice, have cracked off some of their noses and tails. And there's another building on up ahead. It looks to be the office of the groundskeeper, or the sexton, positioned right where the Old Spur Line would resume.

"Am I wrong or is there a light on inside?" I ask.

"Yeah, it looks like they's somebody in there. Hard to tell with them stain-glass winders."

It doesn't stand to reason. Clearly, no one has worked these grounds in over half a century. The overgrowth of honeysuckle, holly, and general disrepair suggest this place has been long abandoned. A glimmer of life, however, flickers within that house ahead.

"I have no memb'ry of ever seein' this place before," Carver wonders aloud.

The little grass-roof building sits in a coppice of pine at the corner of the graveyard. It looks transported from some

Swiss mountainside where alpenhorns and yodeling echo off the Matterhorn. A trackside telegraph wire sags into an opening in the roof.

A strangeness of calm descends. The cloud ceiling lowers and encircles us with a wreathing fog. A cold snap at midday seems odd, but it's been looking like rain for a while.

We bike through another obstacle course of roughage. Limestone, crawdad mounds, and woodpiles. We hop off our bikes and stealthily walk them through the mist and up to the gothic stained-glass window where we detect the deep white-washing sound of static. With only a small bullet hole in the glass to peek through, it is difficult for us to see what's going on inside. But, sidling up, I giver a squint.

In the corner of a dark office slumps the silhouette of an old man dressed in red flannel and suspenders. I see maps and faded charts tacked to the walls. Toppling towers of books clutter the checkerboard floor. Mildew, holy water, and the faint perfume of artificial flowers waft lightly through the bullet hole. Antique medicine bottles twinkle along the windowsills, and the little room is awash in the sunset glow of analog radio tubes. The furious tapping of Morse code is all we can hear now. Carver leans our bikes quietly against the building's hedges.

"What's in there?" he whispers.

"Some old-timer is sitting up in there on his ham radio or something. He must've turned this old place into his radio shack," I reply.

"Weren't you in the Boy Sprouts?"

"The Boy *Scouts*? Yeah. Why?"

"Don't you know what all that beepin' means?"

"Let me see." I crane my head and listen.

RADIO

I was always a sucker for radio. Shortwave, longwave, medium-wave… whatever. It was a relaxing mystery. I reckon it's the one good thing I got from my father. He left a faint AM radio on at night when I was very young. But he kept it tuned between the stations so the signals would flow together and form secret messages. All night he would lay there listening with his eyes wide open. His long white hair unfurled beneath a skeletal frame, his arms folded in an X across his chest.

I didn't need a radio though. If I held my teeth apart just right, I could use my fillings as conductors. Eventually, I'd fall asleep as a mouthwash of voices mumbled in my jaws. To this day I can still tune them in.

Every crash of static. Every garbled communiqué. They remind me of the flickering beacons at sea. Vague indications of distant warnings along the horizon. Wayward, undulating profundities, like electric flotsam and jetsam, fading in then fading away.

Ghostly memories of my father come and go in the same way. Dark, disturbing dreams of trouble, moving between the wrinkles of my brain. Weaving like a copperhead from my right hemisphere of "Love" to the left marked "Hate"… frontal lobes tattooed like the knuckles of a sinister Southern charlatan. I bet it's the same Blood Snake of Brother Stiles' televangelism. Restless as a shark and slithering into the darkest depths of my gray matter.

I have my doubts about the events that led to my father's demise. Do they think I'm a fool? Does Mama think I don't know? It was all something of his own making, the result of the weird company he kept or the peculiar books he read. It was each poor decision, each fork off each crooked path that led to danger. And nothing short of murder! And not some freak work-related "accident." Give me a break.

Brother Stiles

CONSPIRACY

I squint harder to hear the message. In my mind's eye the dots and dashes begin forming a rhythmic synesthesia. I can feel the words forming flavors of sound. I can taste the solder and flux. The tones are deep pulses that resonate in the veins of my mind. Slowly, I begin to comprehend the old man's words. Each completed character builds upon a growing understanding, and now sentences are sliding together to fit into a whole paragraph. What seemed at first to be a random sequence of blips and chirps has become not just information, but intense, arcane knowledge. My eyes well with tears as I struggle to grasp… THE TRUTH!

A pencil on the old man's table lifts to hang mid-air.

"What's he sayin' up on that squawk box?" I can hear Carver ask me through the fog.

My legs weaken beneath me. My eyes roll up in my head. I steady myself with a cedar limb and squeeze its needles into my fingers.

"What's the matter? What's he saying?" Carver talk-whispers.

"Gimme some whiskey," I order in a cracked voice. "Something's going on."

Carver pulls a flask out of his pocket and hands it to me.

"What does it say?"

"I don't know." I take a tug at the bourbon. "It's all in Latin or something," I lie. "Something about the Freemasons. And God and stuff."

"Whoa!" Carver whispers in a breathy state of exhilaration.

"Skitch thinks Freemasons run the world. They kilt JFK and are breedin' a master race using the DNA they gethered from the UFOs at Roswell. They try and trick you by wearin' them funny little shriner hats, drivin' them buggies around in parades. They want you to think they're raisin' money fer cripples but it all goes to buildin' an army of super soldiers they's engineerin' to whoop Jesus at the Rapture."

Carver is out of breath. It's as if he's been waiting to tell me this all his life.

Truth is, I was lying about the Freemasons. I just thought it would distract Carver for the time being. What I actually heard was something absolutely unexplainable. I am at a complete loss to put it into words. But I believe it involves a higher order of spiritual energy, a magnificent darkness contained within this county and inside these woods. A pantheon of powers concentrated in a "Realm of the Red Snake"(?) To explain it any further is to defy the power of mystery… and to expose the limits of language. Who am I to utter such unfathomable heresies? I swear. These words, these notions… they have permanently scarred my brain. Like a branding iron, searing down into a tin of TV dog food.

But the bourbon absolves my worry as the sexton's key falls silent. Yes, this old man, this hobbyist on the fringe-of-the-fringe, has completed his work and sits now in dread stillness. Is he awaiting a reply from beyond our realm?

We agree to leave the dreamy figure to his sepulcher and roll on.

SHORTCUT

Behind the sexton's building, a handcar sits astride a short line of train tracks. The rails lead over to a tipple by a wooded ravine. We discover a dump of cracked tombstones below, each defaced with crooked lettering and typographical errors.

"I reckon he pumps that car over cheer to dump off what he gommed up," observes Carver.

"You can't erase a carving."

"You orta run down there and steal one of them headstones," Carver suggests.

"How would I pack it home? Even the small ones must weigh a hundred pounds. Do you wanna carry…"

A shot rings out.

Carver grabs me and flings us both behind the trunk of a tree. His shirt has been pierced through the elbow, but I see no wound.

"Shit!" he hollers through bared teeth. "I forgot!"

"Who is it?!" I holler.

"Demp. I totally fuckin' forgot. He's the asshole that owns them woods over there. Look! He's got his guns set up in them deer stands. Old bastard kin just sit at home and shoot at us like a damn video game. It's remote control!"

I sneak a peek at the camo-draped deer stand. It is outfitted with a semi-automatic rifle, a rotor, and a single electric eye.

"We'll need to cut acrost that way." Carver points with his chin. His shortcut leads through a seemingly impassible ten-acre thicket.

"Demp is bat-shit crazy. He's usin' real live ammo. I tell you what, he's wound up tighter'n bark on a tree." Carver runs a pinky through his bullet hole, checking for blood.

"Man oh man."

No time to ponder the esoteric message I just decoded. It's time for fight or flight.

"Let's run go get our bikes and head over there. Lucky fer us, them rotors move slow."

At the count of three Carver and I make a break for it and head off in our new direction. Out the corner of my eye, I see the rifle slowly tracking behind us. Four more shots ricochet off some headstones. But headlong we fly, deep into the Kudzu. It hangs like bolts of muslin flowing down from the crooked limbs above. The ghostly forms remind me of the raised arms, hoods, and beaks of medieval Plague Doctors. Soon enough, we are safe within their cloaking embrace.

"They call him Demp," Carver explains later. "He don't want nobody settin' foot or even layin' eyes on his property. He ain't right in the head. Besides bein' crazy, he's all eat up with the throat cancer too, so he's got nothin' to live for. He's gotta fish out his little electric voice-box gizmo just to cuss at ya. He puts it on his throat and makes shapes with his mouth. He sounds like a damn robot offa *Star Track*."

"Yeah, I've seen people use those."

"All he does is sit around spittin' blood into his coffee can. Spittin' blood and shootin' mockingbirds outta his birdhouses. But back in the '50s he was a hell-raisin' badass. He once-t got in trouble for bodysnatchin'! But it turned out he was just diggin' up his mother-in-law's grave to dynamite her bones. I reckon it wasn't good enough that she was already dead."

"Old bastard."

"Yeah. But he always gets away with it. Arson too. He burnt down three houses they was buildin' next door to his property. He got off scot-free with some lame excuse or another. Good thang is he's so mean and unchristian, he's trapped here in The Deadenin'. Unless he wants to lose a year. But I tell ya what, he's slicker than boilt okra."

Carver pauses, wiping the sweat from his forehead.

"Okay, so here's the deal. To avoid him whole, I done cut a trail that T's off the mainline over here." Carver uses a stick to draw a map in the dirt.

"It runs down the side of a bluff, so the path's steep as hell. It comes out at a boat ramp over at an old basin. The lake's all dried up, so it's just a quarry down there now, but if ya ride yer bike down the bluff fast enough and hit the ramp, it'll shoot ya sky-high and right down into that quarry bed. So I hope yer up for it."

"I'm down for anything," I mumble. My mind is still awash with profound misadventure. Thankfully, the liquid courage I just pounded is doin' the talkin' for me. I promised myself a good time and, so far, I'm not disappointed. Slightly shook up, perhaps, but not disappointed.

On past a heap of soiled furniture, Carver hangs a hard right deeper into the blue-green heartwood. He has previously marked the way with red spray paint, but it has grown up thick since then. In fact, the forest is so thick each tree trunk nearly touches the one next to it. A web of grapevines fills in the rest. Each vine hangs slack as a hammock.

"Damn! There ain't enough room to swing a cat!"

"Snaggly as a barrel of fish hooks!" Carver answers back as he and I brandish our swords and get to work. Behind us, our bikes lean upright upon the bushwhacked walls of our slowly forged trail. And with every ten feet of exhausting progress we must go back to get them. Recoiling branches lash our faces, again and again.

SPIDER MONKEY

The tarpaper shack of the "Monkey Man" can now be viewed through the widening gaps. Everybody I know remembers the eccentric old-timer pulling his pet spider monkey around town in a Radio Flyer wagon. He must've ordered the little critter out of the back of a comic book, or maybe it got loose from the Calvert City Circus. Who knows.

But a few years back, the Monkey Man met his match in a single spoonful of potted meat. He choked to death in his La-Z-Boy and sat there for weeks with his satellite TV going full blast and the monkey curled up in his lap. When the authorities caught wind of his death, the literal wind of his rotting, summer stench wafting from the woods, they discovered the body and the pet monkey standing guard of it.

They say that little feller pitched the biggest fit you ever did see, screaming and baring its teeth for three hours and leaving the cops no choice but to shoot it. From the top of the door it fell to the floor and immediately ossified, its tail locked in a zigzag-rigor and its face frozen into a grimace of fangs.

The funeral planner thought it fitting to place the monkey in the coffin with its master; that way they'd be together forever. Now the screeching simian spirit is given to rise at midnight and haunt this area... a corner of the woods now known as the Monkeyshines.

It's a quarter to eleven before the light of day returns, and the path ahead is rockier than I had expected. Slabs of giant limestone resemble a natural staircase. These are the Steppes.

A fox darts out from the recesses of the jutting rock shelters, but once more I am detecting unnatural movement. Somewhere in my periphery I sense the silhouette of a stickman dancing on a fencepost.

On second glance he's gone.

Is it the monkey? Some teenage vampire? Or just another pesky stray jesus?

Chapter Eleven
HARRAKINS

Windstorms from the south.

Stickers snag our britches while we bounce our bicycles down
the rock steps. A clearing blooms through the trees as the light
of day returns.

"Here it is."

Ah, relief from the forest! A craggy white canyon gapes wide
at the sky like the jaws of a screaming planet. From atop its
teeth, we survey the vast sweep of an alabaster quarry below.
It is where, with a little luck and athleticism, we'll soon touch
ground.

A mirage ripples the horizon like the waves of an ocean, but
a panasonic rumble warns of storms. The high prow of a front-
line hulks heavy, flashing a mute code of amber from a hidden
filament. Heat lightning and the flicker of a dying sun. Although
the Sun's copper coin is unredeemed, beams of the eclipse lend
its nimbus around the massive cloudbank in elongated trapezoi-
dal rays. They are cartoonish rays even, like the trademark label
on an old orange crate—or the bars that shoot out from behind
the head of a fearless leader, smiling down upon the mowing
scythes of the proletariat. Stupid, childish bands of light, as if

drawn in magic marker by the infant Son of God. So tack it up on the fridge with a magnet. "Nice job, kid!" says the LORD. But that's just what you say.

"It's been a-lookin' like rain since dawn. Thunder before seven, rain before eleven!"

"Whoa-ho-HO! Take a look out there!" I point with my eyes.

Three white dust-devils descend from the black sky like tentacles in an ink cloud.

"Yep. That's typical. These harrakins come a-blowin' up from Reelfoot Lake every summer!" Carver says with a smile. If we time it out right, he thinks we could launch ourselves off the ramp and into their grip to catch some air. The thrill ride of a lifetime!

"Let's go fer it!" Carver shouts, slapping my back like a gym coach. But he goes first, mounting up at the edge of a two-hundred-foot ramp. Pausing for breath and scanning the landscape to make some last-minute calculations, Carver reels back, adjusts his crotch, and then hurls himself down the rocky way at full speed.

Fists hold fast while arms absorb a jackhammering motion. A small avalanche of gravel follows behind him. Dead ahead, a twister waits in lithe undulation… its slow dance making all the movement of a hypnotic hoodoo woman. Carver barrels forth, like a little juggernaut, pedaling down onto the ramp, up the incline, off the lip, through the wind, and into the tornado's whisking column. It is perfectly timed as the storm's arms pull him inside, deep into the central eye. An extra 15-foot lift draws him Heavenward. It torques him like a propeller blade for three full 360-degree rotations! Then, like a kite that's lost its zephyr, he plummets to the ground and power-slides a swoosh into the gravel.

"Whooooo-HOOOO!" he triumphs with a rebel yell. "Die, Demp, die! Yer turn! Root hog er DIE!"

It's a tough act to follow, but, hell, I'm a little drunk. I ponder the distance, guess-timating the moment my dust-devil will pass. I turn full attention away from my many years of self-doubt and give over to a merciless force: one of lost Southern enterprise and Kudzu hunger.

I stomp the rat-traps and off I go, down the mountainside at top speed, head down and hell-for-leather. My brain dedicates itself to navigating each pit, pebble, and crag, maintaining complete balance and control. My mind's eye, however, follows behind as if outside of my body, looking down and out ahead of me. I hit the lip of the concrete ramp and suddenly I'm aloft to find a twister all my own.

"LORD HAVE MERCY!!"

Harmattan winds lift me in a speckled haze of stinging sand. I am weightless and alive. I can make out Carver's cheering in the background as my body and soul rise within the white windstorm. It is pure adrenaline as I reach the zenith and time stands still.

Has anyone ever done this before? I wonder as my hat gets sucked into outer space. Peppering sand blasts my face and neck, and I'm spinning like a brat in a swivel chair. The tornado has wholly consumed me.

Then down I drop. Down toward the quarry-bottoms below. Down down down. Deciding to go it alone I throw my ten-speed aside and Geronimo my legs, running midair, awaiting impact. The bike hits first and bounces itself into a ditch. But I stick my landing, post-holing my feet into the creek mud with a wet, buckling crunch. I slowly gather my full posture, lift my head toward Carver, and punch two fists of victory into the wind.

"YES!"

"Pretty. Famn. Dancy!" Carver hollers. "You musta plum gone up an extree twenty-five friggin' feet!"

"God dog!" I shout, picking up my bike as the three dust-devils dissipate against the cliff. "That was insane!" My heart is boxing my chest bones, my eyes are crying out sand, and I can tell that adrenaline is masking some pretty severe bruising.

"Did you get as sand-blasted as I did?" Carver asks, showing off some of his bloody abrasions. Black blood congeals around pebbles stuck in his skin. He spits out a mist of grit. Red rivulets stream down his cheeks.

"Yeah, I got popped pretty good, but you were right… it was worth it!"

After some atta-boys, we're back on the loose. The familiar friend of the Old Spur Line welcomes us back. And just like that, I'm sitting on top of the world. Sober as a judge and in love with life.

Chapter Twelve
CARVER

This old boy may be a sissy, but he ain't no pussy. Ain't half them mother-humpers back home kin come out cheer and deal with all this gun-farr and whatnot. Gotta hand it to 'im. Anybody else'ed turned high-tell whence Demp'd come up a-shootin'. And, I betcha, this old boy'd go toe-to-toe with the White Thang if it ever come right down to it, irregardless if he ain't never set a trap or skint a buck. He cain't help he ain't never done none o' that crap. That's the problem when you don't come up with no real daddy. My daddy learnt me all that shit early on. Meemaw learnt me about the roots and I'm thankful to the LORD, buddy.

Poor sum'mitch never knew his daddy, nor all that weird devilworshippy shit he was into. Meemaw tolt us all about it. Said t'watch out for that bad ol' man. Tolt us how he'd come down to Uncle Lee's Flea Market where she had that fortune-tellin' booth set up on weekends. Set it all up inside a teepee so the white folks'd eat it up… readin' snake gourd seeds and stirrin' tea leaves. He come a-huntin' that Mad Stone she worn up around 'er neck. He didn't notice it all tucked up down in her squaw costume, but he started talkin' smart and she tolt him git. He was up to no good. She took her finger and drawed his face in the wet cement of that slab we was buildin' a shed on. "Memorize that face, Carver baby, and steer clear of him. He's a Hoofenogger, part man/part woof, and he'll kill ya dead!" I only seed him in the flesh once't, just that one time... yessir, just that one time. This old boy ridin' his bike behind me, well, he's the spittin' image of that old sum'mitch.

Woof tracks! Speakin' of. Ain't been a woof in these parts for 100 years. Joe-Pye weeds a-bloomin' on the southside bank of the Galilee Swamp. Gonna grab a gob o' that shit on the way back. Make me a po'tice for this flesh wound. Cain't let nobody know I really done got myself shot.

Shee-it. Ain't his fault he looks like his daddy. Look at 'im. He couldn't hurt a fly. Look at him shadowin' me like one o' them fish on a Great Hwite. Bless his heart. He's hungry to learn who he is, but best jest let him study on who he kin become. With or without his effed-up daddy's whiteboy blood.

Honey in the sycamore knot. Looks like a tumor. Hell, looks like a damned ol' tiddy! Man, why's everythin' out here gotta look and smell so sexy?

Chapter Thirteen
DADDY

An unexplained childhood memory.

It was July 3, 1976, and the nation was in the throes of Bicentennial Fever. Small towns unfurled miles of bunting to adorn their town squares, parks, and gazebos. It was like stepping into a Norman Rockwell painting as the "Spirit of '76" took hold of America. Mama, Daddy, and I were on summer vacation, weaving through the mountains of Kentucky like a slot car.

Daddy never liked being away from his Marshall County digs for too long, so he took the curves fast and hard with a "Let's get this over with" attitude. Indeed, every charming roadside scene couldn't be passed up fast enough. There were no stops at souvenir shops. No scenic overlooks. No swimming pools or old motels with neon signs. No national parks. No Smokey Bears. In fact, nothing about this wild ride into the far-flung crannies of Kentucky spelled "vacation." And Daddy seemed scarier than normal. As if in a spell, he kept flooring it, eyes afire with reckless will. It seemed like he was intentionally driving farther and farther away from civilization as he turned from one dark gravel road onto another.

Occasionally he'd pull the car to a stop and get out, leaving Mama and me behind to wonder. We'd sit inside that cramped old Datsun and watch him scuttle off into some abandoned factory or warehouse in the woods. Or this old TVA facility, long left to the ravages of time. Windowpanes gaped with jagged glass teeth. Brick walls spilled in blocky terra cotta crumbles. Trees grew straight up out of smokestacks as fields of ruin ran wild—and formless creeks flowed through it all. My dad skipped and bounced like a madman in a frantic search. He disappeared inside the gutted facility as we waited in the hot car for what seemed all of an hour. I transfixed on his strange movements while Mama just sat there and listened to her tape of The Carpenters.

He finally got back into the car, tossing a red pebble up and down in his hand like a mobster flips his dime. He stuck the thing in his pocket, started the car, and drove us toward town. Had he found what he was looking for? Perhaps. Perhaps not, as he continued to speed along in an evil mood. (But when wasn't he in a bad mood?)

What did my mother ever see in him, I wondered. I asked myself many times until I finally just asked her. One day, in a rare display of candor, she dropped the church lady shtick to let me in on something. Come to find out, before they were married, and long before she had found Jesus, they had dated for about a year and a half. But it was a long-distance relationship. She lived in Kentucky and he was down in Arkansas for work. One night, she was in bed reading when she looked up to see Daddy's face slowly emerging through the wall... his long white hair whipping in a swirl of cosmic wind. It was as if his face was slowly revealing itself, nose-first, through a curtain of space-time. Two seconds later, the phone rang. It was Daddy, calling from Arkansas.

"Did you get it?" he asked.

Mama told me that he'd been concentrating on her that very moment, practicing his "soul travel," in the hopes of impressing her. She was impressed, all right; they got married two weeks later. These days, that kind of display would normally scare the living daylights out of her. That's just how much she has changed since finding the LORD.

Daddy continued to speed along, cutting through the Hazard town square. Then something again caught his eye. The courthouse was bustling with activity, swaddled in a million flags and that ever-present bunting. But Hazard, Kentucky, had gone that extra mile for Independence Day 1976. Costumed teenagers posed like living statues high atop the court pillars that cornered the roof like turrets. (You still see those characters every tax season: teens hired to stand by the road dressed like the Statue of Liberty. Green togas and face paint.)

Evidently, the city had employed them just to stand up there and impersonate the Ladies Liberty and Justice, plus a couple of founding fathers. Silly as it was, it had to be a tough job holding a pose on a pedestal, sweating in the sun for minimum wage. Their upheld torches and scales wobbled in straining poses of patriotic commitment.

Daddy pulled the Datsun to a screeching halt, burst out onto the street, and stood there staring at them with his hands in his pockets. It was a concentrated gaze with a wicked smile. To be sure, I followed his line-of-sight to the target: the young female statue standing nearest to us. I watched in horror as the girl's legs began to buckle, until, finally, she fell four stories to her death. It didn't take long before Daddy had the other three picked off as well. One by one, the youngsters toppled to their demise, cracking their heads and backs on the sidewalk below. It was right then and there, as horror swelled my senses, I understood that Daddy had indeed found what he was looking for.

As screaming crowds formed and sirens wailed like wolf

packs, Daddy started the car and drove us back home in silence. Silent save for Mama's Carpenters tape, which played in a loop the entire seven-hour ride.

Chapter Fourteen
FATHER OF WATERS

An abandoned bridge.
A brief visit paid by a stranger.
Another tall tale from Carver Canute.

At a fairly good clip, we pedal along a smooth section of the Old Spur Line. Tobacco flows in umber waves on our left and right. Each furrow fans past my periphery like the flickering frames of a zoetrope. It is getting near noon but the wind is cool and it's just what I need to keep my mind clear.

"So how much of their bodies can you still see?" I ask, hoping for the most gruesome answer this liar can muster.

"Well, the crows had 'em picked clean years ago, but their bones are wrapped up tighter than a banjer string. So they ain't a-goin' nowheres. They're just a-plum hangin' up there, inter-twung in those branches like a Mississippi Wind Chime! They still got some of their clothes on though, like how them mummies do. They was hoarders, so all their stuff's gethered up in them trees too." Pedaling along with no hands, Carver laces his fingers together to illustrate.

"You know yer there when you see them white-painted tree trunks. It's supposed to keep the piss-ants away. They was talk of havin' a tree service come out there to cut the bodies down, but it's all government property now, so it's been locked up in paperwork since 1977. The house is all cobbled in on itself. Most of the old newspapers layin' around got danged ol' Jimmy Carter on 'em."

I imagine the creepy old Carter-era couple, dying in their filth together. I can see the sinister vinework taking hold and spreading out... festooned with the twisted viscera of legend. It's all quite sad, actually. At least they were together in the end. I should be so lucky.

Oh Delilah, I think to myself. *Why can't you see he's a cad? Remember when he groped your sister?*

"Yep. That stuff grows quick." He pauses. "Hey, what happened to yer weed whacker?"

I look down to discover an empty scabbard rattling against the fork of my rear wheel.

"Crap. I must've dropped it back at the rock pit. It probably went flying when I hit the ground. Or the tornado ate it."

"Don't worry, I gotcher back. The bridge up here done caught far, so we're gonna have to wade across the crick and carry our bikes over our heads. You think yer up fer that?"

THE BRIDGE

Pressing through a patch of weeping willows, we come out the other side into an awesome green arena. It's the grand cove of the outer bank of the Bloodyshin Fork of Clarks River, one of several succeeding offshoots of the Tennessee River. I've heard that, taken in altogether, the waterways form an aerial view of a devil's skull. And if I'm right, this part would be the horns.

The bridge's decking goes only to a point; any farther and there are too many missing timbers to proceed. The fork waters twinkle between the cracks some sixty feet down. And with every step, the ties shift upon their joists, creaking like the hinges of Hell.

But there it is. Towering ahead, obscured in a gale of gnats, it's the old Bayou Bridge. It stands alone, disconnected from the extension where we stand. From this angle its rusty arches seem to rise up like the carrion ribcage of Mother Earth.

The bridge sulks in the languor of mid-day, weeping openly from rusty rivets. Its steel girders are scorched black by the belched steam of by-gone locomotives. Perhaps good ol' No. 801, local history's midnight passenger train, AKA "Whiskey Dick," left these marks. Whiskey Dick was the train that ferried Prohibition-era bootleggers to and from Kentucky's secret speakeasies. Bourbon bottles jingled in the luggage racks as drunken cavorters hung out the windows, swinging their mugs to an off-beat ragtime sing-along. Now U.S. highways have replaced the glory days of good ol' No. 801.

Upended crossties protrude from the riverbed below. They must have plunged from this height and stuck like giant mumble pegs. "Oh, the stories this bridge could tell." But the lazy, good-for-nothin' gal has sadly run her course. We backtrack off the extension and descend the bank.

From the looks of it, some heavy metal stoners must've found this cove back in the '70s and tore it all to hell. Party animals rocking out to Blue Öyster Cult and Sabbath. They must have incinerated some of those planks with their bonfires. But the graffiti on the concrete abutments bear traces of other, even darker characters.

KKK

I picture territorial Klansmen, Satanists, and Kentucky Vampires emerging from a purple fog of psychedelics to leave their markings in graffiti paint and blood. Southern history is, of course, plagued by such sectarian mischief. Night Riders, Loyal Leagues, Rifle Clubs, Red Shirts, and other delta cults, both left and right, forced their will on society long ago. It has always been the case. The hot house of our Southern climate produced many mutant strands of sweaty zealots. The sun fermented their brains that stewed in skulls full of moonshine, fear, and vengeance. But, despite our checkered past, it is interesting to note that the Northern agraria and Pacific Northwest host most White Power activity today.

Facing the desecration, I observe the way vandals have—to quote the old saying—"made no mark yet left a stain."

Because spray paint is everywhere:

S.R. 1980
KKK
3 LEGGED PERVERTS
HAIL SATEN!
RODERICK FERRELL
AC/DC
S.R. '77
TEMPLE OF SET
ORDER OF COPPERHEAD

"Like a briiiidge over troubled teens…" I sing.
These kids formed the loose confederacy of townies that I

always tried to avoid, and avoid becoming. They are like the tormentors who kept me indoors for most my childhood. Stoney Kingston and those Trans-Am-driving metalheads who stole my bike to score angel dust. They beat up my friends in the FFA, and once even shot my dog. Poor thing was just trying to be friendly, but Guff Poat, the star quarterback, claimed he was "rabid and attacking him." It is beyond me why he would think a bunch of cheerleaders at the ballpark would be impressed with him shooting my Irish Setter. But damned if they didn't love him and his muscles even more.

Yes, I resent them all, but, strangely, I owe everything to them. I wonder if they lost a year trying to exit the woods... heathens that they were.

TABITHA

Out ahead upon dry land, we sense the sound of galloping thunder. The blur of brown fur blows by us at lightning speed.

"They she goes!" Carver hoops.

"There who goes?"

"Li'l Tabitha Holt. Out poundin' her trail."

He pauses to spit.

"Yep, I figger she's gittin' on eleven year now. Skinny as a rail. Still cuttin' her own dog trails out here. Ridin' that Great Dane like a pony."

"That was a dog?"

"Yep, she's even got her own little hand-tooled leather saddle and everything. I put 'em around 30/35 miles an ire, at least! That's prob'bly who ya seen back in Carter Mill. Poor thang. She's got a terrible home life. Just terrible! Her mama's one of them hoarders too. Even saves her dirty toilet paper. Crap and all."

"Ugh."

"Yeah. Ain't no bound'ries in that fambily neither. Her daddy diddled her for years, come to find out. No doors allowed in the house. He just tacked up blankets 'cause he done kicked in all the real doors. Front door too. Mud just tracks right in from the yard, splits up into differnt paths and goes off into all the rooms. No wonder she's out here cuttin' her own fresh new path."

"So the daddy's gone now? He go to jail?"

"Nah. He had a huntin' accident out cheer once. I believe I already tolt you about that," Carver winks.

So there you have it. Carver is a murderer.

Tabitha and her dog are long gone now. We can barely see them anymore. The sound of galloping paws and snapping branches grows fainter and fainter.

BAE BAE

Carver squints, spits, tugs at his business, and goes, "Hey, look at this."

"What now?"

"No, I'm serious. Look at this." He points to a tree trunk he's been groping at for the past minute or two.

In the bark of an aging elm is the word BAE BAE carved in a blocky scrawl.

"What's a 'bae bae'?" I ask.

"You don't know who Bae Bae is?!" Carver scoffs. "Bae Bae is a Southern hill spirit that roams through yer dreams. She is tall, dark, and don't speak. She was this perty little slave back in the olden days. Pre-Civil War. The massa of the plantation knocked her up, so, t'keep it a secret, he went and drownded their lovechild in the crick. Bae Bae was so tore up over it she went slap crazy and throwed herself in the crick too. She died and the massa went on about his bidness."

Carver stares off into the past, contemplates his next half truth, and lights up a cigarette for effect.

"Whelp," he snaps the Zippo shut. "He started havin' nightmares and talkin' in his sleep. 'Bae Bae... Bae Bae.' He'd say her name a couple of times. But his wife just so happened to always wake him up right before he said it a third time. And every time he'd wake up they'd both smell somethin' burnin', like hair or oil or somethin'. They couldn't figure it out so they a-went on back to sleep."

Carver pauses to let that bit sink in.

"Okay, so he a-went on back to sleep and started sayin' 'Bae Bae' again. Then he'd say it again. Once-t... twice-t... and on that third time the ghost of Bae Bae appeared with a knife in her hand, standin' over him like a Boo Hag. Her eyes a-clouded over like a Catahoula hound! Well, Bae Bae, she stobbed that knife so deep into her massa's heart that his eyes popped clean on outta his head!"

Carver pauses again for effect, drawing on his cigarette.

"Well, after the wife nearly went nuts from the whole ordeal, she started puttin' all the puzzle pieces together. She figured out her husband had knocked up that no good 'Bae Bae,' so she tolt the house slaves to go throw his dead, cheatin' ass into the crick so that he could be with his whore. So they went and tumped him off the Bayou Bridge. And down he went into Davy Jones' Locker."

"Yeah? Yeah?" I mockingly fish for more.

"Whelp, every midnight on a full moon they say if you come to this bridge and peek down, you kin see the massa's eyes float to the top to stare you down. Then they say 'the Eyes of Clarks River are upon you!'"

The whole time Carver was telling his story, I could clearly see him palming his pocketknife. The blade was dull with the green smear of fresh sap. However, for all of Carver's faults—lying, drinking, cussing, fighting, trespassing, vandalism, and, well, murder—at least it all leads to a good story.

Around us, on the bridge's abutments, train hoppers have left behind some interesting tags to ponder too: *Coal Train, Colossus of Roads, Agony Wagon*. Their graffitied monikers stir images of mystery and freedom. The rest of the area is decorated with old Tab and Billy Beer cans, pop-tops, two soiled mattresses, stray brassieres dangling from tree limbs, and the waterlogged carcass of a skinned buck. Plastic Walmart bags wave like flags, perhaps marking meth stashes, and squeals echo from a distant puppy mill.

We continue to walk our bikes down the clay bank, battling weeping willow roots to keep from tripping. At last we are able to wade into the depths of Clarks River.

"Time to get yer legs wet!" yells Carver.

Deeply bruised from my fall at the quarry, I struggle to keep my bicycle saddlebags high and dry. So I can't resist when Carver comes to my aid, hefting not just his but both bikes overhead, hand over fist. It's a true display of Southern hospitality. Nowise abashed, I appreciate him and tell him so. I'm really starting to get exhausted. Schools of shiners bite at our midsections as we wade on. A water moccasin pokes its nostrils up as it swims by, slick as a ribbon. The cool olive water is refreshing, but I sense there is a shroud over the place. Maybe it's the lush, vaulted canopy that makes me feel small and vulnerable. Maybe it's all the snakes in the water too.

This Bloodyshin Fork reminds me of another foreboding pool of sin, the swimming hole of my youth where outcasts like me weren't allowed. Teenage bathing beauties and their bronze boyfriends would party, get drunk, and screw. One handsome couple overdosed and fell to their death from an outcropping. Mama told me about it at the breakfast table before school and I couldn't help but bust out laughing. Like I did when all those jocks got killed in that car wreck. If only it could've been Guff Poat or Stoney Kingston. Stoney wasn't really a jock, but he sure was handy with the ladies. Telling lies and strumming tunes about his adventures in The Deadening, that's how he wooed

Delilah from me. No matter what I did to impress her, he always found a way of improving on it. My jokes, my stories, even my music, all of it improved upon by this talented liar. Came riding up and swooped her up on a stallion one day. Literally, swooped her up off her feet and onto his horse! How cheesy is that? Why, oh why couldn't it have been *him* that had his head cut off by an 18-wheeler?

Those assholes got what they deserved. Call me "Crap Knife," will they?!

Once atop the west-side platform, Carver stops for another cigarette while we both drip dry. The forest is still faintly humming like a leaky church organ.

THE GRID

I feel like a pioneer out here. A veritable Daniel Boone, forging a trail through the darkness. Or maybe I'm an old homesteader back in the days of "Westward Expansion," the White Man's quest for more American land.

As you may recall from history class, millions of Sooners hit the trail, staking their claim, and, as they did, they rendered straight and true the crooked buffalo trails and footpaths that led them to the Pacific. In the process, they created a sort of grid that divided up this American wilderness.

New property lines and railroads soon criss-crossed the old aboriginal wilds, creating order out of chaos. And, if you stop and think about it, these crosses are quite the fitting symbol for the conquering force of Christianity. For what is a grid but an infinite expression of interlocking Christian symbols?

This American Grid reminds me of another great Wonder of the World, the Native American Nazca Lines. Both the grid and the lines are extraordinary examples of man's ability to carve the land into giant symbols. And both serve as immense ground-displays meant to impress their god(s) upon high. One is rigid and cruciform, the other sinewy and amorphous. But which of the two would the Heavens favor from its LORD's-eye view?

Perhaps it was the White Man's telegraph poles that tipped the scales. Miles and miles of yet more crosses, and their overlapping cables, added insult to pagan injury. The resulting culture clash, as history books record, was not pretty. After shedding much blood, sweat, and sap, both Nature and Native America were sent kicking and screaming into the corner of their new rectilinear confines. It would seem the Heavens had made its decision.

Ah, but you ask, aren't the two of you there to get "off the grid"? Indeed! For look at those crosses now! The barbed wire is all rusty, the railroads are overgrown, and the old telegraph poles trail off in a row of haphazard diagonals. Their arms uphold flaccid, ivy-draped wires, and every other one is betokened with the stamped tin badge of a defunct utility: as worthless as a Confederate coin.

If I squint, I can imagine rotting pale-faces crucified on every pole, creosote dripping down like blood, their American Dream long exploded in their hearts. No surprise though. Pagan Nature, by Design, will always strike her balance. Even today's proud infrastructure will one day be like an overgrown lattice, its grid overwhelmed and its symbols of Christendom broken into a cacography of Cherokee runes.

"They usta give us smoke breaks in junior high," says Carver. "Bell would ring and we'd all go out there, teachers and the students, a settin' side by side, just a-lightin' one off the other. But the dentist says I gotta give it up. I tolt him I been smokin' since I was eleven year old and I ain't a-quittin' now. So to learn him a lesson, right before my last appointment, I ate a whole row of Oreos and didn't brush my teeth."

"Okay."

"So he's over at the sink, warshin' his hands and he comes over and goes, 'All right, buddy, let's see them pearly whites.' So, fer effect, I open my mouth real slow, *mmmmahhhhh*. He looks down, jumps back, and goes 'Holy Shit!' like this…" Carver bulges out his eyes, starts laughing at his own story, goes *Whoo-wee!* And then, you guessed it: three… two… one: crotch-tug!

He likes to play up this hillbilly act for comic effect. And though Carver and his brother live in trailers, the truth is they both inherited a trust fund of their folks' casino money, that old fortune they'd made from ripping back off the greedy White Man. But deep pockets can't buy you an old soul, and Carver's got both. So regardless of the money, he's hilarious to be around, and I'm glad he knows where we're going, because I sure don't. I'm as lost as a gander.

While we're stopped, we grab a quick lunch. Our bicycles come equipped with waterproof panniers to keep our granola bars and cokes handy. I take a swig of orange coke while Carver washes down a power bar with some purple-drank. It'll do for now, since the highway and all its amenities are but five minutes from our trail.

The Old Spur Line picks back up and onward we press, down its labyrinthine vista. A blackened summer mass looms in the distance. Its torrential columns form slanting bars upon the cornrows.

"Won't be long before the government makes corn as illegal as marijuana," Carver surmises. "They'll tax our bullets and steal our guns before they eventually starve us out. Yep, won't be long before all our secret pot fields gotta get rotated over to corn. I already know where I'll grow my corn, and they'll never find it. I kin guaran-damntee-ya."

Mimosa leaves turn up their white undersides like sharks' eyes, opposing the murky backcloth. Greens are always greener before a storm and the air is charged with ions. I can taste each of the little quarks of petrichor in my teeth. A black racer tears off into the underbrush as Carver pops a wheelie.

"It's gonna come a hard rain!" he shouts.

Truer words were never spoken through false teeth.

Chapter Fifteen
STONEY KINGSTON

I was having a hard time opening up and making friends after my father's death. And my mother… well, she meant well. She put me in the Boy Scouts and kept encouraging me to reach out to my sixth grade classmates, make friends and invite them over for a party. Just a little informal mixer. But I knew exactly how it was going to turn out.

Mama was going to slather on her most garish Mary Kay and play hostess (but she wouldn't think to dress up in anything other than her nicest housecoat). She'd try entertaining us all in the parlor, singing her Methodist hymns top volume and off key, chording the plastic buttons of her fan-driven Magnus keyboard, one of those cheap '70s toy organs with spindly Sputnik legs. We'd all have to join hands and sing along to "Pow'r in the Blood" or "There is a Fountain Filled With Blood"… not the most appetizing repertoire for our crappy paper plate dinner: those really, really red off-brand hotdogs and diet Big K.

The kids would roll their eyes and make fun of her—and me—and the messy house that smells like mildew and grief, and her selection of cool "rock and roll music" (The Carpenters). Then I'd watch in sad slow motion as she became self-conscious—embarrassed that she even tried to get us to play those baby games like Pin the Tail on the Donkey and Old Maid. She'd bust out crying and run to her bedroom.

Then the kids would start roughhousing and cussing. Making fun of all our stuff, asking where my dad is. I'd have to play tough and make fun of our things too, even though it broke my heart to do so. The Little Debbie pecan pies that Mama left out for us would get squooshed, and I'd stomp on one to play along, though it would feel like I was smashing my mother's own heart. The whole party would be a disaster.

And that is exactly how it went down. I knew it! But the worst came when they discovered the rusty fillet knife hanging next to our commode. Stoney Kingston was the first to find it. Just my luck. Stoney, that liar I've been griping about, was a buff, loud-mouthed hick who wore his manure-caked cowboy boots to school every day. You could hear him coming a mile away as he clomped his kickers down the hallway, walking on his heels, toes pointed in the air, chin out, butt out, and thumbs hooked through his belt loops. I hated his puppet-looking head and stupid gap-tooth grin. He looked like Alfred E. Newman mixed with Howdy Doody. Of all the people to discover my family's "crap knife."

Yes, we had a crap knife. Our plumbing was so choked by the web of roots from the nearby Deadening that it was impossible to flush our solid waste without helping it along. We kept the knife hanging there by the toilet paper and, after a flush, Mama would always be sure to shout from across the house, "Did you use the knife?"

When Stoney had to go "number two," my mother had to come out of her room to demonstrate how he'd need to chop up his stool before flushing. So, after he was done doing his business, he came charging out to the party, shiv in hand, shouting, "Crap Knife! Crap Knife!"

Laughter erupted and soon the term would become my new

nickname for life. Yes, I still get called that to this day, even Carver knows it. He doesn't really ever call me that though, out of respect. He's a good guy, I wanna believe.

After the party, so shocked was I by my friends' and my own behavior that I confided in my mother that we had stomped all her little pecan pies to smithereens. I felt terrible and cried for forgiveness. How could I be that easily turned against her sweetness? How could I be that heartless, insecure, and impressionable? I buried my face in her robed bosom and begged for mercy. And in that sweet Southern accent she hushed my tears… but told me how those pies, without this week's coupons, had actually cost her a small fortune.

Chapter Sixteen

ONE MISSISSIPPI...
TWO MISSISSIPPI...

The storm descends.
New friends are made.
A Dock Boggs tune.

The harrakin front line has caught back up to us. Windswept branches claw the air like a gesticulating fascist, or Adolf Hitler himself, casting wild his spells in the throes of the most diabolical of diatribes.

Folks call lightning storms like these "frog stranglers" since they're strong enough to drown anything with webbed feet. The looming black hull of its battleship will soon collapse under its own weight and soak us to the bone. There is spider-vein voltage scurrying along its massive bow, and bolts of the stuff ready to crack us in two. We need to find shelter. Now.

High on ozone, we crank along the rail grade with our eyes peeled for a barn, a shed, or a silo. Any port in a storm.

The wind wags the willows as the forest is bled to the color of bone. The warping lens of the atmosphere tweaks the Tint Knob of Nature, bending all wholesome Christian colors out of sight. It's as if we are cycling through a daguerreotype of destruction. Sepia dust and grit whip through the air and into our eyes.

But in the new electric calm comes the strangest visitor from around the bend: one single red balloon.

THE CALM BEFORE THE STORM

Bouncing along, the balloon strikes an eye-popping, hard-candy contrast against the bleach of birch. And, oh, how it does my ol' heart good!

It's just hopping about, blowing lightly on the wind and dangling a small folded note at the end of a string. I'm about to catch it when five to ten more balloons appear from nowhere, equally as red, equally as lost, and swirling about my feet. As I stoop to scoop them up, we notice still another fifty to one hundred more hanging about eye-level throughout the woods, all of them in the slowest descent.

It's as if they're in a stupor, sleepwalking through the calm. We awkwardly maneuver around each one, angling our shoulders left and right, careful not to disturb them. Soon hundreds—no, thousands!—of balloons have joined us, filling the landscape with bulbs of bright crimson. We briefly forget our need for shelter and come to a full halt within the event. They bring an oddly cheery, brief relief from our chaotic day.

"What the hell?" Carver says, finally breaking the silence.

I pick up one to examine the note.

"JUST SAY NO!"
TOPEKA 4H
KANSAS STATE FAIR

"Whoa. That's five hunnert miles away!" Carver marvels.

"Folks must've set 'em loose at the fair and they got sucked up into the jet stream. Man, they've come a long way."

The first drops are starting to fall and, buddy, they are fat! Time to move. Our two-man peloton knows no bounds. We gotta find shelter fast or it's hell-fer-certain. Off we go. Pedaling hard. A distant air raid horn begins its Doppler wail. It sounds like a soprano staked in sacrifice to the Kraken.

We're really bookin' it now. Our tires roll like hoopsnakes! Full tilt and pumping down the Old Spur Line.

Fig. 3

Hoopsnake

SILO

"I hear music!" he cries out through the rushing headwinds. As usual, I do my best to keep up.

I hear music too.

Splat. A giant raindrop gets me right in the eye. Then come a dozen or so more pint-sized whoppers to soak me good. We determine that the music (a fiddle?) is coming from a rusted-out old silo on Obert Kessler's land. A couple of trail bikes are lying in the grass outside by a pile of empty paint cans. Quickly determining that the old-timey music must be coming from someone friendly, we ditch our ten-speeds mid-transit and make a mad dash for the entrance. The bicycles go crashing off on their own.

With a whoosh of wind, rain, and heavy respiration, we spring ourselves upon a young couple inside. They leap back, dropping their musical instruments to their sides, and we apologize immediately. I figure they must be in here "woodshedding." Well, they were rehearsing, until now.

"Beg yer pardon, y'all!" Carver introduces us, shouting over the deafening din of rain on tin. "We's just tryin' to duck out of this gullywarsher!"

"No worries!" says a young cowboy, silhouetted by a gas lamp and tipping his Stetson. "I'm Fang. And this is my wife, Cat!" he points to his bashful blond wife standing all of five feet tall.

"I believe we've howdied once before but not really met," says Carver. "I know yer grand-daddy."

"Yeah, he lets us play in here. We're just bonin' up on a few tunes before our gig tomorrow in town. We come out here so we don't drive him crazy!"

They seem remarkably at ease given our sudden intrusion.

"Well, don't let us stop you!" I shout over what must now be golfball-size hailstones.

"All right, then. It'll be nice to have an audience. Tell us what you think."

Fang signals to his bride to flip the switch on a certain gizmo over by the door. It's a bit of Rube Goldberg ingenuity, a clockwork contraption. As it putt-putts to life, it appears to be a mechanical drummer they've invented. I stoop and squint to inspect it. The motor of a sewing machine turns a wooden whirligig, which in turn pivots a combat boot that kicks a wash-tub. It all runs off a buried extension cord that leads to the house. Cat cranks up the tempo with a rheostat.

"Maybe you'll recognize this one! It's a tune from where I grew up!" The two start in on an old chestnut that I instantly recognize: a sea chantey from the Alabama coast. Fang's voice, quite pleasant actually, recounts the story of Joe Cain, the daring young fellow who brought Mardi Gras back to the streets of Mobile. The words recount the exploits of his "Order of Myths," a defiant krewe of funeral-plumed revelers who paraded aboard a coal wagon in the face of occupying forces.

Oh Jooooe, the shipyard's dried up!
Your suit's torn and matted
And you're looking mighty rough!

Sensing a neighborly spirit, I pull out my trusty Cracker Barrel harmonica and jump in. Sure enough, I rightly guessed the key and am allowed to join the jamboree. Fang nods his head upon the chin-rest and belts it out while Cat strums along on her fox-tailed mandolin. She grips a smashed penny for a pick and trills the long, held notes. It's a glorious acoustic phenomenon as the instruments blend in with the pelting hailstorm, and I am transported to the tin roof patter of my summer long ago with Delilah.

It's crazy where your mind travels when you get lost in a song. I remember the sound of rain on her tin roof, of that cooling mist that blew in through the window to bathe us in the bed, of how it seemed to activate a tangy bouquet in the house: one of pheromones, coffee stains, and antique furniture varnish. And as we lay there in the serenity, forehead-to-forehead, she would play for me the tunes she was catching in her fillings. And she taught me how to do the same for her. She was a mystic, and I know the symphonies she sent me were not of this world.

Yes, Delilah Vessels, herself, was the sensual summation of all such intangible magic. Heartbreaking whiffs of nostalgia and music… yet somehow wild and hyper-sexually charged at the same time. Great God Almighty! But unfortunately now for the both of us, she is ceding these gifts by courting someone her inferior—planting her flag into the Stone of the King.

The Cajun tune ends with a big collective laugh and some small talk about Fang and Cat's little farm. I can tell they're old souls, trying to recreate the better parts of the past. I like them already.

"Y'all three sound good together!" Carver proclaims, slapping his hand on my shoulder. "You sure you ain't never jammed with this old boy before?" He is flabbergasted that complete strangers can interact with such unspoken ease. One-liners, profanity, and whiskey have always been his social lubricant.

"Nope. Never."

"Well, hearin' y'all makes me happy as a dead hog in the sun," Carver hollers, shaking his head with his hands on his hips. "I mean, how do y'all even do music?"

"How do we *do* music?" Fang asks. "Well, it's a funny story actually. Me and my two brothers never dreamt of hittin' a lick until this one night when it come up rainin', like how it is now. Lightnin' struck the house and sent a shiver through the air. A ghost shiver. But it kinda felt good. Ever since then all three of us got into this singin' and playin'. Ain't that right, Cat?"

"M-hm."

"So where are y'all headed out in all this mess?" Fang asks.

"Have you ever heard of the Kudzu House, that place with the bodies up in the trees?" I answer.

"Yep. I've been there once. And it is real. But let me just tell you. Don't go on Old Man Demp's property. He tried to kill me once."

"Yeah, take a look at this!" Carver says, showing off the bullet hole in his sleeve. "The old bastard took a pot shot at me just today! So we took a shortcut to cut around his place. Ended up catchin' some air in the harrakins."

"Dannnng! Well, that's good, because lemme tell you," Fang takes a breath. "If you keep down this here Old Spur Line, there's a little trestle that belongs to Demp over there. I figured it was still safe. Government land and all. But I figured wrong."

Above the soft wash of rain, Fang relates his close call with Old Man Demp, a tale that begins with one foot set smack dab where it didn't belong, where the KEEP OUT signs had been hidden by bracken.

Fang describes the twenty-miles-worth of razor-wire lacing, re-lacing, and looping around Demp's massive militia compound. Red Confederate and yellow Don't Tread On Me/ Culpeper flags hung across the rotten wooden walls. Racks of elk horns hanged lynched upon the planks.

"Demp came bustin' out with his shotgun, goin', 'Keep off mah property!' Then he spit a wad of bloody chaw right in my face. I took a hard kick to the butt, fell, and split my orbital socket on a train rail. And I still can't get the sound of his throat box out of my head! Thank goodness I was able to hobble back over into the woods where the Klepners live. They patched me right up."

"You mean that old German couple that lives in the midget house?!" Carver shouts for some reason. "Aw hell, are they still alive?!"

"Yeah, the dwarf couple. 'Little people,' I reckon they prefer to be called. Their house is so awesome on the inside. Low ceilings, tiny rooms, itty bitty furniture. Well, Mrs. Klepner, bless her heart, she got out the first aid kit and Dr. Klepner sewed me right up."

"They saved your life, didn't they, hon?" Cat chimes in finally.

"They sure did. My head had lost a lot of blood from the fall, but they patched me up, fed me, and told me to steer clear of that whole area. So I haven't dared go back since."

Fang in the house of the Little People.

"Probably fer the best," says Carver. "Demp ain't playin', boy. He's an ornery sum'mitch."

"Do you know 'Danville Girl'?" Fang turns and asks me.

"I can fake it."

"Y'all go ahead," blesses Carver. "I couldn't carry a tune in a bucket... no matter how many times lightnin' struck me. But I kin play the hell out of a stereo." Carver pauses. "Y'all don't mind if I smoke, do ya?"

"Knock yourself out," Fang winks.

The Alabama sawyer peels off his first lick. *Sonofabitch I'm taaaaarrrred!* the fiddle seems to sing. And we all roll in. And buddy, it's a barn-burner! Why, you can almost hear good old No. 801 plowing down the rails one last time.

> *Look up, look down that lonesome road*
> *Hang down your head and cry.*
> *The best of friends sometimes must part,*
> *So why can't you and I?*

LIFT

It's a good ole jam that rocks on and on. At one point we even achieve what Irish musicians call "Lift." It's when the pickers are so musically connected that their chairs seem to lift up and the floor falls away. It's an ecstasy few achieve, but, from my view, we are hovering here some ten-odd feet in the air. Now we are in the slow carousel motion of a candle-powered Halloween lantern and I can't get down. And I don't want to get down! I am honored this sensation has come to me. Below us, the rhythm of the drum contraption sets Carver's goatboots to cloggin'. "It's flatfoot dancin'!" he shouts as a ghostfinger of ash bounces an inch off his cigarette. Dust kicks up from his feet and into the shaft of kerosene light, encircling us above. Its auburn flicker casts long devilish shadows across the silo walls, illuminating our floating bodies and dangling boots. There's a wiccan quality to the whole scene, as fiddle music inside a harvest tower recalls the rites of Salem.

Alas, all good things must come to an end as we descend softly toward the ground. "Danville Girl" concludes with a double "shave-and-a-haircut" ending and we stick the landing as if we were longtime bandmates.

"Har har har!" Carver's belly laugh shoots his cigarette across the room. Overcome with joy and banjo-eyed bewilderment, he swats his knee like an old-timer, slaps me on the back and goes, "Shoooo, brother! I didn't know you could blow a Nigger-Whistle like that!"

Awkwardness immediately fills the room. Raindrops snicker in the new silence as the drum contraption putt-putts to a stop. Fang and Cat drop their eyes in shame. That kind of language doesn't fly in here among these good Christian folks. And that is as it should be, of course.

The embarrassed couple stares at the ground while I nervously babble about anything to fill the silence.

"Pardon my French, y'all," Carver offers. "I reckon I got carried away. But really, y'all. That sounded really, really good." Carver's voice trails off in a rare display of guilt.

"That's okay," Cat pardons. She is detecting Carver's tiny mind but good heart. That or his ethnicity. Perhaps her own buried white guilt over smallpox-infected blankets and the genocide of Native America has saved us for now. Either way, it's a pleasure for me to be in the midst of such smart, sensitive people, especially in a world infected by quite the opposite. A little more small talk and all seems forgiven.

"Well, I suppose it's safe for us to get outta here now," I conclude.

"We'd love to come see y'all play at that festival tomorrow."

"Please do, it's at the Coon Dog Cemetery," says Cat. "Y'all have a good time finding the Kudzu House. That sounds real fun."

"Bring your harmonica tomorrow," says Fang. "Let's do it again!"

Chapter Seventeen
DADDY Part 2

The home I grew up in was practically all windows. Zero curtains. At night, the house lit up the neighborhood like a lantern. Mama must've had an odd aversion to drapes—or having to dust them—so our every move was visible to the outside world. Daddy mostly kept himself hidden in the basement while we moved about upstairs, bathed in 100 watts of blinding light. It was so bright, in fact, at night it turned the inside surface of our windows into a House of Mirrors, so there was never a way of discerning any movement that might be stirring outside.

One evening, a strange fancy little man paid us a surprise visit. (Of course, we didn't see him coming, or anything else outside for that matter.) He rapped at the door with a brass-knobbed cane and demanded to see my father. His red vest and cummerbund bulged beneath a black tux and tails, and his slacks tapered into a pair of spats. He had a round face that seemed frozen into a broad castle-toothed smiling crescent. I put him as a cross between Teddy Roosevelt and a chubby Guy Fawkes mask (what with his pencil-thin Van Dyke beard). And his squinchy eyes were as thin as stabbings.

"He's a bad man," I remember thinking. "He's got skinny eyes." His voice was low but insistent, so my mother made haste calling Daddy up from his lair.

Once the two men were face-to-face, a loud argument broke out. But the little man never stopped smiling. I heard my name bandied back and forth, but I was too young to understand the conversation. The door slammed shut and Daddy told us to shut off all the lights and get to bed. I did exactly as he told me. I ran to my room in a panic and tried to go right to sleep. I stared outside at the stars for comfort, but it all just looked too large and random. It's as if every star, planet, or pinprick of light had been sneezed there from the nostrils of God. The thought of eternity only made matters worse. Suddenly silhouetted against the stars was the shape of the little man stepping into place right outside my window. Despite my calls for help, the odd fellow just stood there smiling down on me in the pallid starlight. Again, I whined and called out for my parents, but they never came. And no matter how long between uneasy fits of eventual sleep, I would still wake to see him standing there—his unyielding mad gaze forever fixed down on me.

At some point during the restless night, more visitors assembled in the yard behind him. They ambled in a loose gathering, stirring like shadows cast by the moon and remaining there, or in my dreams, until the break of dawn. I must have finally fallen asleep from the weight of sheer dread.

My father had his tragic "accident" the next day. Yes, he was finally dead and gone forever. The victim of "workplace negligence," they said. But I suspect foul play—from the strange little man and his lurking companions.

My father's last words to me were something he screamed from his room that horrifying night. His answer to my cries for help:

"SHUT THE FUCK UP AND GET YER ASS TO SLEEP!"

Chapter Eighteen
WUNDERKAMMER

An exodus from the forest.
"Local color" described.
A startling discovery in a forbidden place.

For a good five miles we've avoided any fallen trees or washed out bridges. The storm has long blown over and taken its red balloons with it. Now we are left in a sluggish haze of humidity and mosquito swarms, and it sure would be nice to grab another coke.

We trek off our path for a quick break. Bottom Road is an old access road that will lead over to Elva, Kentucky, about a mile away. Civilization is slowly starting to return, but, like Carter Mill, time and the elements have left many a shack standing in crude mismeasure. "Danville Girl" still plays in an endless loop in my head like a dusty 78. I consider it the perfect soundtrack for our trip into Forgotten Kentucky.

"Up here is Elvie-town, where my uncle sold moonshine. This is where they found that murdered family."

"Another *legend*?" I use my fingers to make air quotes.

"No, I swannee to the LORD, this un's true." Carver's voice

lowers to a somber deadpan. A rusted sign marks the lonesome whistle-stop of…

ELVA

"They discovered the whole family murdered here. They were draped up in the tree limbs, covered in blood."

"God. Don't you have any happy stories?"

"You really wanna hear a happy story?"

"Nah."

"So… the only one alive was the youngest. A six-year-old girl. They found her sittin' in the grass below all them dead bodies, just a-singin' and a-playin' by herself in the blood drippin' down from above. All devil-may-care. Everybody thought she was evil, got skeert and runned away. They were so disgusted by the sight of that little witch they couldn't get it outta their heads. So the whole town swore a pact that they'd keep the place hidden. Sho 'nuff, no one's ever found it since. It's called 'Secret Mountain.'"

"How do you keep a mountain secret?"

"Aww, I'm just bull-shittin' ya. That story's counterfake as hell!"

"Really?"

"Maybe," Carver pauses, "but then again… maybe not. Up cheer's the old Elvie four-stop."

GENERATION GAP

We stray farther down the road. It's more a graveled easement owned by some local yokel, back-porch gawkers. And no offense to Carver, but I put the "tooth-to-head" ratio around here at about 3:1.

Squalid hollers and trailer parks are strewn with broken toys, deflated plastic Christmas globes, flat tires, and dog crap. And I think to myself, *What the hell happened to "Southern Pride"?*

Obstinate Scots-Irish blood! Still revolting against the sophistication of its royal overlords. Now it's left them vulnerable to the seduction of low-brow identity politics and slacker-chic marketing. Redneck antihero belligerence in place of the hard-won pride that farming brings. One dead-eyed inbreed hangs stretched-armed from a low tree limb, his bare feet just inches from the ground. His slump-shouldered son stands drooling below, poking his daddy's bare ribs with a pointy stick.

"Wudder y'all lookin' at, assholes?!" the three-year-old shouts at us. His daddy just hangs there like a gibbon, stoned and drooling.

"Mind yer own business, Toodie, you little bastard!" Carver hollers back. "That little shit-head's gonna be trouble one day."

I'm appalled at how much these morons contrast to the senior citizens just across the alley. I can see the old folks at home, watching from their porches, tsk-tsking the way their world has changed. Why, it's as if these two generations aren't even of the same species.

Barn-quilts adorn the old folks' outbuildings. Perhaps they use these hex symbols to ward off the evil spirits of Gen-X sloth and Baby Boomer decadence. They were, after all, nailed there by the "Greatest Generation." They are the folks that had once built a dignified post-war country with their own two hands. They fended for themselves and stoically did what they had to do to survive the Dust Bowl, the Depression, and the War with the Huns. They went around putting things down, doing what they had to do. And the more I think about it, the more I believe those old bastards had something there. And what they had was a life packed with hard-earned meaning, a life more in keeping with the Bronze Age than with this new so-called "Information Age." But, again, I digress.

On up ahead and in a crisscross motion, one of these old octogenarian hellcats rides her lawn Snapper. Her wig dangles from the handlebars as she waves hello.

"You boys comin' from the warter?" I think I heard her ask.

"Yes, ma'am!" I shout above the engine noise.

"Well then! Watch out fer them woofs down by the crick. They'll gitcha!" She gestures in a grabby-grabby motion with her creepy old talons.

"We'll be careful!"

"It's the dawg days of summer! That's when they'll gitcha!"

The old lady spins her mower in a fleet 180, laughin' and a-wavin' good-bye. Sassafras, scallions, and mint shoot out from under her blades and the whole yard smells like a salad.

Beyond that, trails of garbage bags and whiskey bottles lead past a "scrap yard" where someone has spray painted over the *S* on the sign. A lonesome cur sits chained to a Confederate flagpole out back, surrounded by electric barbed wire. And then there's the failed video rental/tanning salon by the main road. And yes, it's one of those "shut-down-because-the-owner-was-videotaping-naked-women" kinda places.

MANAKINS

Now we are passing the cabin of Keith Atkins, Marshall County's resident visionary "folk artist." Atkins, in an effort to glorify the days of Route 66, has converted his yard into a campy roadside attraction of outsider art, scrap metal, colored lights, and kinetic water fountains. He calls it his "Hillbilly Garden." And it is a mess!

He is perhaps more famous for having recently fought City Hall and won. Accused of creating an eyesore by the Elva town elders, Keith faced them all in court, decked out like a Snuffy Smith cartoon hillbilly, just to tick them off. Representing himself, he successfully argued his First Amendment right to junk up the neighborhood as he saw fit. Now "Hillbilly Garden" is sevenfold the blight it once was, with corrugated tin, hand-painted signs, muffler men, and Kmart dummies strewn six ways from Tuesday. His revenge story even made it onto national news.

With victory securely his, Keith currently spends most of his time baiting the sheriff with sight gags and roadside mockery, painting signs like "Pot Garden, This Way ⟶"—a bad pun that leads to a field of half-buried crockpots, skillets, and pressure cookers. He's a hoot, I tell ya. And the Constitution of the United States of America is on his side.

While passing his front porch—a still life of posed dummies with weather-beaten clothes and wigs—I am reminded of the one unifying peculiarity of all Southern folk artists: their unceasing affinity for mannequins!

I ask you, gentle reader. No, I beg you! What is it with plastic mannequins and visionaries of the American South?

I've seen it time and time again: mannequins, body-snatched from department stores, whimsically dressed-up and positioned on porches like grandpappies, or set in the driver's seat of broken-down vehicles, or roped in the trees like lynched angels. It's supposed to be cute but I find it unceasingly disturbing. Maybe it's the anatomical correctness of it all, or the comfort level these artists have with dead eyes, frozen smiles, and stiffness. Perhaps it's the way they like to dress them up and pose them. It just has too much of a serial-killer-lite feel to it all.

I find myself distracted by the matte gaze of one particular dummy on Atkins' porch. Plastic deadness encases it like a human decanter. (Does real flesh-and-blood scream from within?) A sheer muumuu swaddles around its ball-jointed frame, revealing the sun-faded, hardened rubber of its hips, arms, and neck. Kids have scribbled ballpoint pens across its dry-rotted cheeks, and' a mussed wig of yellow doll hair sits askew on its head, looking like a rained-on owl. Cocked metal rods, like leg braces, run down into a pair of bunny slippers, and the whole thing looks like it's been violently bent into a rigid Z, just to sit there crooked forever on the porch.

As if caught in a magnetic pull, I follow the vague thousand-yard stare embalmed behind the dummy's black eyes. I am utterly captivated! Yes, I am floating along a slow course set for the depths of those dead, dark portals. But just before I am sucked inside... lo and behold, it blinks! My feet slip off the pedals and I gasp. Indeed! IT IS NOT THE DUMMY! I AM THE DUMMY! Yes, its eyes are those of a real human being. Keith Atkins' hatchet-faced mother-in-law, as a matter of fact.

Bless her heart. Saddest thing I've ever seen.

FOUR WAY

At the junction of 999 and 1210 is the FOOD OWL, a country store that sells Chester-fried chicken, 86 Octane gasoline, "pipin' hot" tamales, and lotto tickets. There's a rusty Red Man Tobacco thermometer from the 1970s nailed by the entrance and a tin door-pull embossed with the logo of a defunct bread company. It's a picture of a smiling Beaver Cleaver-lookalike having a sandwich. Although we've only been in the woods a few hours, it's good to see signs of civilization again. Carver stops in for some Camels.

"You still want a coke?" he asks.

"Sure."

"Leaded or unleaded?"

"Do I look like I'm on a diet?"

The screen door squeaks open and slams shut on its spring-action hinges. "Hey Dolly!" Carver hollers. The obese woman at the counter turns away from her judge shows just long enough to mug the look of indifference. No nod hello, no nothing.

A pit-stained gray XXXL DALE JR t-shirt hugs her toad-like figure. No doubt some NASCAR t-shirt cannon fired it at her years ago. "It's free, I'll wear it," she must've said smugly. Well, it's better than the one she usually wears. The one that reads:

There's a food counter in the same back corner where a make-shift Goodwill booth is set up. Grade D beef, Mexican bathtub cheese, and secondhand clothing make the whole place stink. It's a mix of sweatpants, tacos, and feet. I hang back for some fresh air, sticking my head into the ice machine outside by a roadside Vietnam vet. He's waving an American flag and sitting on one of those aluminum walkers with a built-in potty. That thing you hold yourself up with or stop and take a dump in.

After a while cooling off, I see Carver come bounding down the wood slab stairs. A cigarette bounces in his green teeth as he tosses me my coke and flips a wooden nickel to the old soldier. It lands perfectly in his begging hands.

"Don't spend it all in one place!"

Leaning in to him, Carver adds, "Personally, my grand-daddy tolt me never to take no plug nickels a-tall."

The drunk vet squints his sad eye at the token.

"You might wanna giver a chomp. Make sure it's the real McCoy." Wink wink.

"Hey. Don't be a jackass," I say, trying to keep from cracking up.

"Taker easy, hoss. It's fer a free cup o' coffee."

"Thanky, sir." The veteran goes back to mumbling insanities at passing cars and waving his tattered flag. Each torn stripe blows like fringe in the wind.

THE LODGE

"I'm so hungry I could eat the ass end out of a rag doll."

Carver's only dietary restriction is that it "ain't fancy" or "high fallutin'." In fact, it must be Fallutin'-Free. He slurps down his tin of KELLY'S BRAND PORK BRAINS 'N MILK GRAVY and chases it with a coke. I hork down my Zagnut and a bag of VALU-KIST brand HAWG CRACKLINS.

Now that we've got some protein in us, it's time to back-track down Bottom Road. Past Toodie and his brain-dead daddy; past the barn-quilt and the lawn-mowin' granny, and all the tumped-over grain bins that lie belly-up in the cornfields. But over along the edge of the returning Deadening, a certain three-story cinder block building stands alone and vulnerable. Its backdoor... ajar!

The old Masonic Lodge.

"Well hell hell, lookee there. We gotta go sneak inside."

"Hold on. You mean break into the Masonic Lodge? What about their blood pact? Remember Jack the Ripper? You of all people should know the Freemasons take a blood oath to pro-tect their secrets, for cryin' out loud."

"What's that mean?"

"It means they'll kill you if you tell anybody what they're doing."

"Naah, we'll be okay."

"Well, you don't know that, Carver. I'm sorry but I'm not gonna risk it."

"What, are you pussin' out on me and goin' home?"

"No, but I'm not going in. I hear these guys are into some dark shit."

"Well, find your own way to the Kudzu House then, buddy. This is what's happenin'."

What can I do? He's the boss. So we head up to the courtyard, past a rotten rick of firewood, a pyramid of stacked lead pipes, and some old porcelain Gulf signs. A cane-back chair sits pitch-poled off the porch. The steps are littered with unswept leaves, cobwebs, and dead spiders curled into arthritic claws. Sections of gothic wrought iron fencing lean against the banisters in a rusty heap. They have zigzagging lightning bolt spearheads like you'd see in a horror movie. Under the overhang, an ancient Edison bulb still burns from a dangling wire.

After hiding our ten-speeds behind two burn barrels, Carver unsheathes his slingblade and we make our move, climbing the stairs onto the back deck. I feel naked without my machete though. I have nothing to protect myself with should a crazed Grand Poobah pounce.

Dirt daubers sculpt their earthen channels in the overhang (even though it's been painted "Haint Blue" to confound their nest-building). Carver swings back the storm door and we are in like Flynn.

Asbestos, dust, and dirty little secrets whip into our eyes with the onrush of dry wind. The darkened hallway is quiet save for the floor timbers that crack like bones with each step.

It reminds me of all those other odd abandoned places we drive by daily. I mean those back-alley shells-of-buildings you always have to wonder about. Trees seeding up from the gutters, windowpanes weeping black bilge down stone facades. Or those derelict doublewides that sit crooked at the edge of the woods, crammed with hoarded garbage, creamed by the elements, and crowned with snapped aerials. And what about all those failed businesses on the other side of the tracks, the ones with graffiti and weeds but whose lights still kick on at night automatically, giving off an alien strobe through the cracks? And no one knows who's paying the bill or how to shut them off.

And then there are those other forlorn spaces, places that never see the light. You imagine shouldering your way into the tight squeeze of a blocked door, pressing past all the cobwebs and into the shadows.

Your eyes adjust just barely enough to discover another doorway. But you need to move some boxes out of the way for it to open too. There's a stairwell on the other side that leads you farther and farther below, into absolute darkness, stifling heat, and suffocating must. You plod down the crooked staircase, toward a faint impending energy. And though you can feel the horror growing in your body, step by step you feel you must push. Down, down, down into phantom red terror; your eyes are electric, but your smile is painted-on and false. But be a man, I say! Give yourself over! These are the factories where nightmares are made!

"Okay. I'll man up."

"Yeah, it's nothin'. It just smells like bingo in here. Whiskey, smoke, and panelin'. Plus, they only meet once-t a week, buncha old farts. Trust me, we're just gonna have a quick looksee. So they's still plunty time to get to the Kudzu House and back before sundown directly."

The hallway leads past a cloakroom where green glass heads model a row of red fezzes down a long hallway shelf. A row of ruby-and-gold-colored robes shrug on a coatrack. The cowls of kings. Carver hangs back to ponder the symbolism chain-stitched in the sleeves while I proceed into the holy of holies… pulled in by both curiosity and wondrous dread.

CABAL

My mind's eye swells within the sudden expanse of the inner sanctum. Full fascination is drawn inside, the way smoke curls to fill a room. I step in to find layers of dust covering over cryptic intent as mystic symbols are revealed under swipes of the hand. The place feels haunted by a thousand dark rituals.

"What do they do in here?" I wonder aloud.

There are rows of pews like you'd see in the arcade of a cathedral. They all face a stage where candles would be lit. I can just imagine the hooded congregation, ensconced with a common dark purpose. No doubt they join hands in concentric circles and chant. Do they do so for good or evil? Or is it just to impose place memory onto the negative space surrounding them? Forming a virtual tree ring of Yggdrasil itself, cleaving notches into the very Tree of Life?

Yes, I'm beginning to believe that these eccentric menfolk, these sons of the Templars, are the ones really running things. Too many American presidents have been Freemasons. Too many crooked Southern politicians too. And this is their gathering place. This is their community.

But the Devil sits upon the dais…

I approach with reverence, tiptoeing in a hunch. Dim footlights illuminate the chancel here, suggesting this building is still operational. Gnats swarm in the glow like a field of electrons.

Basking in the faint incandescence sit three mahogany thrones, facing outward with looming presence. There is fury in their framework, anger in their carvings. Rough-hewn details along the legs depict screaming demonic faces. Each twisted figure upholds the next character, like a German Expressionist totem pole. Up top, tin globes, representing the Moon and Earth, flank the velvet headboards. They swivel upon each stile like an orrery. Surely they must symbolize how the heavens, in turn, orbit the mind of God. The largest throne occupies center stage confronting a warlock's pulpit, whereupon the biggest Bible I've ever seen hangs heavy in its sacrificial leather, cracked open to the Apocrypha of Judas.

How could they leave this place so vulnerable? I wonder as I scan the room from the stage.

The All-Seeing Eye gazes down from a gold backdrop in the nave. It's like the watchful eyes that swirl in the birches. Or even the eyes of Carver Canute, when they flash psycho.

I return my attention to the altar, and to a little golden nameplate put there by the craftsman:

BROTHER EGGNER METZ
ORDER OF COPPERHEAD

I recognize the name! He was the old German "wood butcher" who got caught making church furniture out of wooden implements of capital punishment. Things like decommissioned electric chairs and lethal injection gurneys. He went around scooping them up as soon as the state outlawed the policy. Why, he even had a scrap pile of century-old gallows wood in his backyard. I read somewhere that the Church of Christ ran him out of town. Accused him of blasphemy. They claimed he was responsible for sawing the steeples off of churches for extra wood. They said he'd admitted getting the idea from a demon, a disgruntled "fallen angel," one that had had its own wings sawn off in Heaven. The demon had taken its revenge by inspiring Metz to do the same to steeples.

True or false, one thing's for sure: the Church meant to ruin Eggner and his business. So he closed up shop and sold his property. But, by the looks of things, he must've stuck around long enough to pick up some extra work with the Freemasons.

Inside his ominous altar I find mostly a mundane pile of nothing: some used Kleenexes, a candle, a pack of Big Red gum. But I do discover a mysterious contraption hidden in back. Cleft from mahogany and slightly smaller than a breadbox, the thing comes stamped with another Metz nameplate. It sports a smooth lathed handle and a dainty drawer of black and white marbles. I assume it is a ballot box for "casting lots." When swiveled by the handle, a marble issues through a hole and onto a plank. It seems I have rolled a black one.

Whose fate is decided by this gizmo? I wonder.

"Hey, come look at this!" I holler to Carver down the hall.

No answer.

"Of all the places for him to start messing with me," I mutter.

I descend the podium and skulk back to the hallway. Luckily, there's some light at the end of the corridor where we had entered. I gather up all my courage and proceed, walking softly so as not to creak the floorboards. Or, worse yet, try not to fall into the terrifying nothingness of what the basement must be.

I am midway down the hall when I swear I hear a shadow. I turn my head and see a robed figure. Like a beast, it springs itself upon me in a wild X. It screams and flails a steel blade that figure-8's inches from my face. I try to holler but the thing has me throttled, forcing me hard against the wall. There's an explosion of copper in my mouth as my back cracks the plaster. The shelf of glass heads and fezzes crashes to the floor. In my panic I am able to upswing two praying hands between the arms that choke me. I force them apart and bring a knee into the demon's gut. I am released. Adrenaline has saved me for the split second I need to plan my next offense.

I gasp and discover it's only Carver, dammit. He's wearing a stolen robe and fez and holding his machete. The hallway erupts with out-of-breath laughter.

"I knew it was you!" I lie. "You still scared the hell out of me! Take that thing off and let's get the hell out of here."

"Man, you got me good! But you look like you just 'bout shit yer pants!" he snorts, adjusting his junk. His laugh sounds like a donkey call.

"Hold up," Carver laughs, still recovering from my knee to the gut. "I wanna go check the rest of this place out. How wuzzit? Did you find JFK's brains?"

"No. You jackass. Run-go check it out real quick. It's not that scary. Just a bunch of weird furniture."

"I'll be right back. Wait for me. I wanna show ya somethin'."

Carver jogs down the hall, floorboards buckling under his goatboots. I make for the door, where the sky is lit with saffron again. Five minutes later Carver returns.

THE CLASSROOM

"Well, you were right. There ain't jack squat down there. That big ol' Bible was cool. Too big to fit in my saddlebag though. But did you look in there?"

"Look in where?" I ask.

"I swear it ain't another trick. Trust me."

Carver walks me to the other side of the hall where the door to another room stands ajar. With a slight push it creaks open, echoing into the expanse of a tall-ceilinged classroom. It is filled with stale air and squalor and dimly lit through old ambered pull shades. Unfamiliar forms fill the floor.

"Whoa," I whisper.

"Look in the middle," Carver notes with a raised eyebrow and spooky reverence.

Giant ceiling tiles have fallen from the weight of rainwater and insulation. They are left in a hanging position, suspended midair by a tangle of wiring. Black mold creeps up the walls and rats scurry about. The cold terrazzo floor is littered with random forsaken filth: wet books and clothes, a stack of unused .

Styrofoam coolers, a box of old work gloves. The room stinks of asbestos, neglect, and decay.

Then I look down and pick up a stray guitar cable.

"Cool! I can use this," I muse, musician that I am.

"No, got-dangit," Carver whispers. "Look in the *middle*."

I squint a little harder.

Beneath the spilling ceiling tiles lies an amorphous pile of something organic on the mattress. Rolled up in a blanket, looking like a blob, it's... a body? Or... a glob of mush?

Is Carver tricking me again? It's hard to tell. My pupils swell with adrenaline as my neck hairs stand on end. Now I can see.

A deformed corpse lies in a rigid lock of rot. The ravages of time have collapsed its face into a gaping moccasin. Spanish-moss-looking hairs form a wreath around its mouth as it silently screams. Its shriveled eye-holes look like puckered leather navels, and what's left of its nose is the ace of spades. It curls its claws beneath a purple chin and peeks its head out of a swaddle like a ghoulish Downy baby.

Drywall dust and bird droppings form a crust on top, and the whole body looks so old and hollow you could almost go pick it up with one hand. Pick it up like a frozen tarp and pitch it like a Frisbee. In fact, it is so far gone even the flies aren't interested anymore.

Regardless, this grinning beef-jerky mummy must've been someone. It must've had a name! It must've had a family! Through disbelief and intrigue it finally dawns on me. Our Masonic Lodge is not so much some Southern gothic funhouse as it is a crime scene! A pall of gooseflesh descends. A swirling chill. Hyperventilation. Then from the depths of my soul comes an explosion of buried religion. Yes, through the lips and past the gums comes bursting forth the mighty name of "JESUS!" Not as an expletive but as an involuntary open rebuke of this sinful sight.

"Jesus! Is that the guy you shot in the woods?! Tabitha's

daddy?!" I shout. "Jesus, Carver, I hoped to God you were just kidding!"

Carver just looks at me surprised and shakes his head. "I tolt you these Freemasons mean bidness."

"No, I told *you*, dammit! Jesus Jesus Jesus!" I profess again, slapping my forehead.

But in my other hand I feel a tug. My guitar cable whips out straight on its own, yanking here and there like a magic leash. I drop the thing but it hovers for an unnatural second, thrashes my legs several times, and falls to the floor.

We both take off running. Rounding the corner and out the backdoor until we hit sunlight. Straight as an arrow, the cable shoots past our ears. A folding chair is sent hurtling at our feet next. With a clanging thud it sticks a landing in the mud just inches away. We scan for more trouble.

"Who else was in there?!" I scream.

"NOBODY!" Carver hollers, obviously frightened with his eyes wide and white.

"Forget this!"

The Tuvan tones of the woodlands roar like laughter. Carver starts to laugh too. His green teeth are bared but he sounds fake and full of wild worry.

Holy God, I am utterly lost in an onrush of questions. Within that pregnant, suspended second between the slice of the knife and the arrival of pain, I know I'll forever be held. Disbelief collides with belief. Then comes the disbelief that you now believe. For it is one thing to suspect the supernatural; it's another thing to have it confirmed.

Chapter Nineteen
SIN EATER Part 3

It's not like he respects this town and wishes us well. Heartless bastard. I mean, he literally has no heart! He only does it to survive. Look at him. Now he's scrambling into the treetops of my mind, scurrying along the planks he nailed there for a hasty getaway. Slow and steady, like molasses running down a butter knife, he rappels to the forest floor on a blackjack vine. He sneaks a peek left. Then right. Then left again. He slithers through the pampas grass, emerging with throbbing eyes. With a hop he's aboard his secret, sacred podium: an antebellum whipping-post lost to time in the misty woods. An obelisk of inglory. Dangling with the chains and shame of slavery, it is a focal point of bad juju. Here he basks in the LORD's reinvigorating light to receive his daily charge. To review today's menu.

Before long, the cursed scavenger is backtracking down the trail, snapping thicket underfoot. Soon he'll be worming back into the hole beneath his shed to sit at a table of plenty. All manner of delicacies await: cakes and pies, cookies and fruit, soups, salads, hams, beans, grits and casseroles. They all line the length of his latest victim's body. A closer look through the candlelight and behold! The victim is ME! My sins, it seems, are "Today's Special."

The Sin Eater says his grace, but his eyes remain open and . fixed on me. The "me" that is watching myself. He sees that I'm spying from above through the catawampus floorboards, but he refuses to break eye contact. Yes, he is staring a hole right through me!

Then, with a sickening twinkle, he curls his grin of crooked teeth. A yellow un-flossed mush of sin-on-the-cob.

BOOK TWO:

PANDELIRIUM

"It was pandelirium! I thought we'd be killed or even worse. I looked out the window in time to see the chicken's coop go right over our roof! All I could think was, Caroline still has my casserole dish!" —Jeff Foxworthy

Chapter Twenty
BURKEHOLDER

Carver's Aunt Glennis.
A visitor from on high.
Separate ways.

QUESTIONS

Quickly back aboard our bikes—rattled, shaken, and on autopilot—we book it down to the Old Spur Line with our thoughts on what we just witnessed. Carver has doffed the robe but is still wearing the red fez he stole, making him look like an escaped hurdy-gurdy ape.

He swears to God he had nothing to do with the body.

"So…" I stammer.

"So, what?"

"Should we call the cops?"

"Hell no! Like you said, we don't want them Masons findin' out we was snoopin' around. Come on, let's get on down to the Kudzu House."

"Hey, man. One dead body is enough for me today. I just wanted to come out here to have some fun. Now this?"

"I ain't askeert of much, but when it comes to the Masons, the ones that are way high on up and in charge? Them's the ones that's got this whole world rigged. Killin' people and framin' witnesses is just what they do!" He pauses. "Here, have some whiskey."

Carver tosses me his flask and I take a deep stinging pull. I try to forget the terrible mysteries of the day, the very mysteries I've been waxing poetic about since we got started.

Thus far in life the closest things I've seen to "the paranormal" are the shocking stunts my daddy once pulled (but those weren't real, were they? I was so young!) and, of course, Brother Withers levitating at a revival. He claimed whoever had "mustard seed faith" could do it too. Maybe it was just a cheap trick, but it scared the hell out of me and kept me godfearing and churchgoing for another four years or more.

And, oh yeah, there was today's visit to the sexton's office. And those shrunken heads? More glimpses of the unexplainable. Lest I lose my mind, I chug a mouthful more of whiskey and attempt to change the subject.

"Well, so much for your theory that once you enter The Deadening you can never leave. Or at least that you lose a year when you do. We just rode right out and got a coke." I suspect I'm just trying to make myself feel better. Trying to quiet this terror.

"Yeah, but we had headin' back into the woods in mind," Carver argues. "Maybe the woods kin predict yer plans. Let you come 'n go as you please, just so long as it knows yer a-headin' back inside. That makes it not count. Plus, I didn't check today's date on the paper back at the FOOD OWL, did you?"

"No," I say, wishing I hadn't brought it up.

I might as well face up to reality. These woods are haunted as shit. Pardon my French. I don't like to cuss but hey, it's true… and I'm a little drunk now. Plus, it's like I heard Brother Tazewell say once: "There's nothing indecent about the naked truth."

ENTROPY

Onward we push to the Kudzu House, standing on the pedals and coasting toward the green oblivion. Stars are made by the spaces between the leaves overhead. Constellations too, if you connect them with a dotted line. They plot out all new mythical heroes and beasts... a whole other cast of our own Dixie-fried characters. It's Daniel Boone instead of Orion, John Henry instead of Perseus, the White Thing instead of Capricorn, and Legba instead of Cancer—all cloistered in the clouds of our windswept canopy.

Pinpricks of light shimmer the way planets do through an atmospheric lens. Or gleam like the knowing, winking eye of our "wise fool" archetype, that Southern singularity who casts his pearls of country brilliance before the educated fool, just as points of sunlight are cast down here to sift through the dust in diagonal bolide rays. Like a shower of comets, they land at last to twinkle up from the trail bed, the lower hemisphere of this giant, sparkling portal where the Southern Cross tilts to form the Confederate X. It is a forest-green galaxy full of primitive life, alien ticks, and snakes, that when taken in altogether is to be respected, marveled at... even feared. Eternally dense into inner space yet ever expanding its Kudzu province without, the vaults of The Deadening occupy an echelon neither micro nor macro, but perfectly sublime from our humbled perspective. The wake of Carver's trail-powder whips it all into nebular motion. A swirling Coriolis of dreams and fears.

And now ghosts!

We must muscle our bikes through the thicket near the cabin of Carver's Uncle Earl.

Poor Uncle Earl seems to be in worse shape than we are. He is out back by the doghouse, duded up like an urban cowboy and fumbling for his midday moonshine. He'll soon be aboard the swayback of an old gray mare, a horse that, back in her day, was the pony to bet on. That's what everybody said. But not anymore.

Earl's ten-gallon Resistol is brand spanking new and slightly too big for his head. It pushes the tops of his ears down like a dog. And his paunchy tucked-in rodeo shirt makes him look like a pregnant pencil.

"All hat and no cattle," Carver muses.

Uncle Earl moseys about, fiddling with his leather tack and looking like a rejected singing cowboy from the '40s. We crack up and it feels good to laugh. To laugh for real, finally. But our smiles fade as soon as he climbs into his saddle. It's a sad sight to behold. There he begins to sit in the blazing sun for what Carver says will be hours, brushing his horse's mane, getting drunk, and crying tears of loneliness.

"He ain't been the same since Aunt Glennis left him all alone with that blown-out ol' racehorse. They had a lot of luck way back when, won the Preakness even! Then they got married. But when the luck run out he found out he was hitched to a bitch! Yessir, unequally yoked in the *headlock of wedlock*, ha ha! All she did was sit around naggin' him and paintin' her dad-gum fingernails. And not her real fingernails neither. After that farmin' accident, all she had was little nubs fer fingers. But she'd paint 'em up anyway. Fake little red fingernails at the end of each nub.

"Well, Earl, that poor sum'mitch, he went off t'work one day and left the CB on in the kitchen. Glennis got to talkin' on it and runned off with some trucker. Handle was 'Squirrel.'

"She came a-crawlin' back though, and he let 'er back in the trailer. But the old biddy up and died of brain cancer a few years later."

"Let's leave him be," I suggest.

So onward we press, pedaling hard to put some space between us and the Masonic Lodge. Three mangy blue heelers come scampering down a dirt embankment that's been piled up to the tin roof of a woodshed. Now they're nipping at our boots. I quickly glimpse how someone has carved the word COPPERHEAD into the woodshed planks. It's the same word that was on the Freemasons' pulpit. But I don't see any snakes around.

"Git!" Carver shoos. "These dogs got AIDS! I knowed the owner. Chester the Molester! Went to California so he could marry his 12-year-old son. He liked to bofo these here dawgs too."

The dogs snarl and buck with each kick to the face. Two of them squeal and give up.

"I forgot to tell ya, speakin' of crazy Aunt Glennis. She had a blue heeler. Uncle Earl used to tease her about that dog. Any time it made a peep, Earl said it was just barkin' at the voices in 'er head. Funny he said that because it turnt out it was smellin' 'er brain cancer. Dogs kin smell cancer, y'know. In fact, that dog damn near saved 'er life with all that racket, kinfolk takin' notice the way they did. But it was too late. The cancer was too fur along. She died and Uncle Earl hain't been the same never since. He thought it'd be sweet if they buried her next to the doghouse. Like some kinda got-dern Disney movie. But, wouldn't you know it. That damn dog went and dug up her skull and runned off with it! He was still tryin' to get at that cancer!"

"Gawwd!" I say, channeling my laughter into the bike pedals. Thighs are burning. Push, man, push!

"I dated a gal that had a blue heeler too. They's good dogs, my favorite breed now. Don't let these bastards fool ya. YAH!" Carver kicks the last one in the face.

"Got to know her dog. How long did y'all date?"

"About a month or two. She wuddn't much to look at, but she had some tig ol' bitties. And she could gob the chrome right off a trailer hitch, boy! Whoo-wee!"

Hmm, I figure I'll have to marry the first girl I find who likes chasing ghosts and riding bikes around out in the woods. Someone who, with only the rarest of qualities, can share with me the music in her *teeth*. That shouldn't be too hard to find, right? Maybe I can still talk Delilah into dumping ol' Stoney Kingston. That lying, cheating sack of crap.

The final AIDS Wolf offers one last snarl and goes snooping off into No-Man's-Land.

HUNCHBACK

Pedaling on, we pass a trackside placard commemorating the fatal flood that took the lives of six Amish children. The horse and buggy were washed off a bridge after a downpour in 1997. I remember the story well. It was in the paper. This is the place they named "Ghost Ditch."

Chinquapins and gumballs pop under the rubber weight of our wheels. Patches of cattails—more like cat o' nine tails—lash our legs near bloody. But we're making headway now. There's a pot-bellied hopper car capsized in the ditch up ahead. From here, it looks to be graffitied by some rail riders. *Conrail Twitty* and *Virginia Zeke*.

We're off to check it out and…

SMACK.

Like a bomb, a brown smudge whips down from on high and Carver is thrown to the ground.

"Aagh!"

I hop off my bike in a panic.

I run to meet him and discover his monkey fez and the top of his head are covered in excrement. The sounds of squealing laughter, more plopping matter, and bizarre noises bewilder.

"Get outta here! It's Dooney!" Carver points upward. Looking fifty feet up I behold the naked undercarriage of a grown man defecating from a tree limb. I barely miss getting hit myself.

"Got-dammit, Dooney! I'm gonna KILL you!!"

The shrill squeals of this Dooney fella curdle my blood like a catfight heard at night. I can see him now in his Elmer Fudd hat.

He is gathering up his britches and escaping along a wobbly path of planks nailed throughout the canopy. I know I have seen him before. Him and his planks.

Whoever he is, he's a scrawny little booger, missing some bones in his neck and possibly a chromosome or two. Some gas-huffer, I reckon. Yet I marvel at how he uses the bouncing of the timbers to spring gracefully from tree to tree, like a hunchback leaping along the vaults of a cathedral.

I return to find my befouled friend toweling off the mess with a t-shirt and some canteen water. But no amount of cleansing will be enough in so many, many ways.

"I am gonna kill that idiot!" Carver is the maddest I've ever seen him, and understandably so, given that he was just, well, shat upon.

"I thought I saw somebody out there." I gasp. "That fella's probably been following us since Carter Mill. Who is Dooney?"

"Ughhhh! Dooney Burkeholder. Great grandson of the feller what owned all this property years ago. But Dooney's no count. He's just a mute-ass sum'mitch! Bastard cain't even speak, but everybody feels sorry for him." Carver sings that last part with sarcasm.

"He's just some sawn-off, funny-lookin' maniac. They gave him a job at the fillin' station. Always forgets to put the gas caps back on before people drive off. They let him wear a gold robe and sing in church too, but he just moves his lips. Hell, he cain't even say his own damn name! But for some reason they even went and made 'im an orner-rary deacon! He just hangs out at church all the time havin' people feel sorry for 'im. But he's dad-gum plum filthy! If they only knowed he was goin' around shittin' on folks in the woods! Got-DAMMIT!!"

Carver keeps angrily daubing the filth out of his hair. Fat green-eyed flies are starting to pelt us and the smell is just punishing.

"Ughhh. I gotta run back over to the crick and warsh off. You see which way he runned to?"

"He went south, I think? Looks like those crazy bunch of boards run northwest to southeast." I check with my compass. "Yep."

Carver bikes back to the nearest bend in Clarks River while I hide in a patch of widow's tears. I'm buzzing and paranoid yet exhilarated. I carefully eyeball the treetops for any more trouble. However, it seems I've come to nest in a furious plat of poison ivy too. Our state bird, the mosquito, makes its appearance next. There's a swarm of 'em. Then chiggers, fire ants, and humidity all join in. Yes, The Deadening has set about to torture me here in my hiding place. But I will grin and bear it if the alternative is getting pooped on by Dooney.

Chapter Twenty-One
SERPENT

Skitch Canute.
A dangerous development.
Psychedelic consequences.

In this misery of bug bites and allergy symptoms, my mind travels to a happy place. To memories of my bittersweet teenage crush and the masochistic savoring of pain and melodrama. Back further to my days of childhood in a safe home with Mama. The major scales and high gloss of youthful optimism.

Melancholy and sentimentality too. Warm glowing candles and hymns sung around the Magnus organ. Close-knit family get-togethers with Grandma and Grandpa, and other wistful recollections of my country home. The welcoming golden glow envelops me as I bounce around on the parlor furniture. I am young, almost weightless, and happy; I can smell the nostalgic bouquet of bacon and coffee. Mama's organ music echoes like a heavenly music box and I am safe and innocent for now. Daddy's dead.

I remember when Delilah took my innocence in her college apartment one night as the wind blew through those lace curtains. I was so in love with her messy black hair, her slightly put-on cosmopolitan accent, and her free spirit. I could tell she wasn't all mine but I didn't even care at the time. What a body! I was transfixed! And for that one beautiful summer I stayed with her, she was my home.

My refuge now will be the pastel colors of her vintage kitchen cups, her collection of medicine tins, and the overflowing ashtray beneath the wind chimes of her sundeck. Soft winds would whistle across the glass lips of old 7Up bottles lined along the rail, and the hum of their odd-pitched notes joined in with the chimes above. The days were bathed in the most heavenly light. With pinks and golds, it cast a sadness far heavier than the grayest of skies. And although this mantle remains, perhaps, once all this is over, she will welcome me back with that strange love we left behind.

It's time to stop kidding myself. It's time to stop thinking that Nature is beautiful in all her "many forms of intensity." Buzzards and bones and death and Dooney; I'm sick of it all and I want to go home. You can keep your grays and browns, your stagnant water and impenetrable wilds. Away with self-inflicted pain! My throat is constricting. My allergies inflaming. I've seen one too many dead bodies for the day... for an entire lifetime! It's not funny anymore. Life is real.

> And the son said unto him, Father, I have sinned against heaven, and in thy sight, and am no more worthy to be called thy son. But the father said to his servants, Bring forth the best robe, and put it on him; and put a ring on his hand, and shoes on his feet: And bring hither the fatted calf, and kill it; and let us eat, and be merry.
>
> —Luke 15:21-23 KJV

I commence building my nest in the thicket. Pushing leaves and sticks out of the way. I just want to sit here and hide until Carver gets back.

Jeesh, what would I do without that guy?

I have no skills out here. My father left me vulnerable. All I remember of him is blended with those impressions I somehow received from beyond the cradle. For in the days, weeks, and months before I was conceived, I must have existed as the "twinkle" in his eye. And what set me there a-twinklin' was not just his lust for Mama, but a sinister intensity—one perhaps as old as our shared bloodline. Sure, I was just a tiny window-shaped glint, sparkling there in his retina. Peering out like a candle through a pane, set there in vigil. But even as such a little glimmer, I saw how he was: a man who had nothing good to share with his one-day son, and nothing to share with the world but darkness. So it has been upon me to find my own mentor. To make my own friends.

Enter the Canutes…

SKITCH

I first met Carver and his insane brother, Skitch, ten weeks ago at a Hickman County roadhouse. Honky-tonk music and stale smoke hung in the air as Carver announced to the crowd it was his birthday. Skitch sat back in silence, wearing sunglasses indoors and holding his hand over a match flame. "Like they do in them movies." Carver bought a round for the whole bar, I figure with all that inheritance, and the jukebox blared:

I like my women just a little on the trashy side.
When they wear their clothes too tight and their hair is dyed.
Too much lipstick and too much rouge
Gets me excited, leaves me feelin' confused.
And I like my women just a little on the trashy side.

By the end of the night the two siblings, plus Carver's new-found girlfriend—some honey with tribal "ass antlers" tattooed above her butt cleavage—needed a designated driver. Out of some tweaked sense of duty/adventure, I offered to drive the strangers. So away we went into the night. Skitch sat shotgun while the two lovebirds dry-humped in the backseat. What had I gotten myself into?

It was a long, tense, awkward drive into the darkest country night. Roadside memorial wreaths marked each breakneck curve. Skitch just sat there, petting his holster and staring face-forward like a seething Texas gun nut. The only sounds were the cicadas outside and the shameless manhandling going on in the back-seat. I opened the sunroof to grab some white noise and fresh air.

A few miles into my demented midnight run I heard the unmistakable sounds of coitus coming from the backseat. Sure enough, the rearview mirror confirmed Carver's sweaty naked butt bobbing up and down. That's when brother Skitch inexplicably snapped to life, spun his head around and started high-fiving his brother's backside. Smacking it and hollering "Whoo-Hoo! Git it, boy! Git it! Shoot that thang!" Then he whipped back around, rolled down the window, and started fir-ing his gun into the guardrail.

Seconds later the odor of Carver's seed hit the air.

"NO! Lord, no!" I screamed. "Not in my car!" I swerved to the shoulder. "Get out! All of you! Dammit! I can smell that back there!"

"Hey, that ain't me, man," Carver answered back. "That's just them come-trees a-blowin' in through the sunroof. They just stink like that!"

Skitch nodded silently and poofed the gunsmoke from his barrel like a bandit.

That night warped me for sure. But ever since, I've only wanted more. Call it Stockholm syndrome, or whatever you

want. Maybe I've always played it too safe. These feral person-
alities give me some dark thrill, something I need. Whatever the
reason or "daddy issues," it has unfortunately led to this moment
of misery. I would've loved to been born as simple-minded as
Carver and his ilk: not a worry in the world and dumb as a box
of rocks.

VENOM

In my rummaging through the fallen leaves I disturb a sleeping
pit viper. Twin pricks and the sensation of tiny jaw muscles sink
into the meat of my thumb. It sends me howling with panic.
I reel as the serpent recoils into a hoop and hisses. The vilest
language I know flows in a steady stream. Surely Carver heard
me and will come a-runnin'.

Lub Dub. Lub Dub. The serpent slithers into the blear as the
hot pinpricks throb. I can feel the viperbane burn and spread
fast, and I need to think quick. What to do, what to do? My arm
is stiffening and I am walking in stupid circles. Blurry circles.

Once to my bike, I fumble for anything to bleed myself with.
No knife, no nothing! Invoking God, I curse aloud, swearing
up and down, turning the air blue. Why didn't I go back for
my machete? Carver took both his machete and his pocketknife
with him. Like a feeble kneeling child, I begin to saw at my flesh
with the dull rusty bicycle chain.

"YOOOO CARVERRRRR!"

The Deadening mocks me with a long sarcastic echo. Where
is he? Surely there's a cure he could fashion from some Indian
root, some ginseng or something. Some panacea.

Lub Dub. Lub Dub. Didn't he tell me he had his grandmother's
Mad Stone? That petrified piece of deer cud used to suck the
poison out of bites. Didn't he say he brought that with him? Or

is it still around the throat of old Granny Canute, the midwife and root doctor of their reservation?

Snapping to, I unzip my Carhartts and grab my belt to fashion a tourniquet. My throat and eyes are swelling shut as the venom sears through my veins. My face is pallid and palsied with the pangs of death.

I yell for Carver again and wait for a response.

Only the drone of the woods, howling louder and louder in my head.

"DOOOONEEEEEY!" Hell, I'll give it a go. Who knows?! I'm desperate at this point and wouldn't turn down help from any given inbreed.

No response.

mad stone.

Chapter Twenty-Two
OLD KATE

Queen Mab of the Mire.
The Kudzu Couple discovered!
Dooney Burkeholder.

The sky clouds over yet again. Round two.

Sunlight beams in from the west as showers sail in on a zephyr, and the Devil is beating his wife. Rainbows with bizarro anti-colors refract through the charging ozone. I can taste strange new hues. Or is that just the copper tinge of death? As the rain begins smacking the rail grade, I slip to my knees, wet with sweat and cradling my arm like a baby as it clenches into a dead black fist.

A spirograph of starlight shimmers behind my eyelids. Heavenly geometric shapes swirl like interlocking fireworks patterns. Shapes form into faces and, in a split second, I see everyone I've ever met fanning past my mind's eye as if flip-booking through a stack of photos. Within the split-second span of a card shuffle I can somehow appreciate each and every individual face.

Now I am back-diving into a cave of stars. Everything here is made of millions and billions of dots. They dissolve away, reassemble, dissolve away and reassemble again, forming an entirely new locale... a mystic, mercurial replica of The Deadening.

A perpendicular universe.

It's starting to rain and rain hard. Tin sheets drop like guillotines as the flood zone swells and swells. An inky deluge gushes in violent waves and surrounds my ankles. But as the black storm passes, a figure emerges from the center of a hovering orb of swamp gas. A flat-bottomed boat and its hunching deckhand drudge forth. I can't take my eyes off her. I dare not take my eyes off her.

She paddles her ferry ever closer. Through the crepuscular gloom I see... a witch.

She stands on the deck of a boat named *Copperhead*, pulling a long forked stick, and not a ripple is left in her wake. Her hair is stringy and stuck to her face. Bonnet tassels dangle down the front of her threadbare flour-sack robe. It clings to her wet chest where her breasts sag like dog nuts. And it sounds like she's humming "My Old Kentucky Home" in a minor key.

She's as ugly as a mud fence, and with each advancing pull through the pea soup the old gal gets even more hideous. She's like some old gnarly root doctor with warts, whiskers, and a brown cigarillo chomped between her silver-capped teeth. Her body is rotten. Green meat stretches beneath translucent skin, flesh the color of a used condom. A red checkerboard pattern flashes in the milk of her corpsy eyes. Is this a sign of demon possession or is she a demon herself? Most likely the latter. Oh yes, she is a demon herself! The very famous demon of Red River, in fact!

The Bell Witch!

I immediately know I'm in trouble.

"Oh yeah, yer in trouble, boy," she cackles as her boat shifts its weight; a ballast of skulls clocks together.

Four Mad Stones of different shapes and colors dangle from her leather choker. Her voice gurgles in her throat like a hot mess. She is undead and cold as a snake.

THE BELL WITCH OF TENNESSEE, that invisible agency of Adams, Tennessee, is no peach. "Old Kate" made herself famous in the early nineteenth century when she began centering her "black events" around one Mister John Bell, Esq., and his family. They say she first descended like a spring-heeled Jack, landing upon the rooftop of the family manor at night, clacking her hooves on the shingles like a satyr.

She chose them for reasons unknown to the community, but rumor has it, it was due to a recently disturbed Indian mound. Even Bell's friend, President Andrew Jackson, verified claims of the haunting. He publicly criticized the demon for terrors he himself endured while visiting the estate. Therefore, he is the only U.S. president to go on record and vouch for the existence of the paranormal. Jackson even organized a band of witch hunters to confront the old gal and subdue her, as is chronicled by one descendant of John Bell:

> "Try again," exclaimed the witch. "Now it's my turn; lookout, you old coward, hypocrite, fraud. I'll teach you a lesson." The next thing a sound was heard like that of boxing with the open hand, whack, whack, and [Jackson's witch hunter] tumbled over like lightning had struck him, but he quickly recovered his feet and went capering around the room like a frightened steer, running over everyone in his way, yelling,

"Oh my nose, my nose, the devil has got me. Oh Lordy! He's got me by the nose."

Suddenly, as if by its own accord, the door flew open and the [witch hunter] dashed out, and made a beeline for the lane at full speed, yelling every jump. Everybody rushed out under the excitement, expecting the man would be killed, but as far as they could hear up the lane, he was still running and yelling, "Oh Lordy." Jackson, they say, dropped down on the ground and rolled over and over laughing. "By the eternal, boys, I never saw so much fun in all my life. This beats fighting the British!"

—from *The Bell Witch of Tennessee*
by M. Ingram, 1894

At present, Kate is way upriver and far, far away from her present-day home in a Tennessee cave. Far from the old Adams, Tennessee, schoolhouse, the home of the "Bell Witch Opry," a weekly commemorative music jamboree in the small town she made famous. Every Saturday night the locals pick bluegrass tunes and cakewalk with the shadows of her memory. But if they could only see her now, tying off her boat with a slimy rope, they wouldn't sing so pretty.

"Yeah, yer definitely in trouble, boy. Definitely in trouble. Trestpassin', cussin', balsphemin'. A-hangin' onto things what don't belong to you. Haw Haw Haw!"

She is pure hate and there is nothing but pointy-eared evil in her words. But I am at her mercy. Despite the tourniquet, my arm is swollen and blackened with poison, and my system is starting to shut down. But I'm still not certain I am truly here. Maybe I'm really just at home, dreaming in the safety of my own bed. Or maybe I've been pumped so full of Carver's horror stories (and even old Brother Withers' *religion*), I've become entangled in a vine of lies.

But no. I snap-to and find my throat truly in the crux of the witch's forked staff. She's got me pinned to a cypress knee and her minions are tying me up with rope. They are masked imp-like little bandits with grotesque gap-toothed smiles. "Hoptown Goblins" perhaps, up from the Red River of Hopkinsville's cave system? My eyes cloud over in their sockets. Although groggy and in shock, I am able to observe my deviant surroundings. Perching on every branch, every sloping bough, and hunching in the marsh are thousands of bizarre characters, seemingly transported from a Hieronymus Bosch triptych.

OSMOSIS

In western Kentucky, we are taught that our waterways are akin to conduit. They carry the electric traffic of spirits and have done so ever since the Second Day of Creation. Genesis 1:7 states that water flowed both below and above the firmament, on Earth and in Heaven. This means that watery climes are where spirits originally came from and where they will always prefer to be. If you don't believe me, take a ghost tour past the brick alleys and wrought-ironed balconies of New Orleans, Savannah, or Charleston and see for yourself. The lapping tide-waters upon such famously haunted ports act to transubstantiate water-borne wraiths into thin air, where they may then freely move about within our realm. It is a fascinating cycle that is perpetually occurring, just like the processes of osmosis, evaporation, or precipitation. Yet, all the while, we blindly go traipsing through their midst. Traipsing through the troposphere of our strange haunted planet.

> Then went the devils out of the man, and
> entered into the swine: and the herd ran vio-
> lently down a steep place into the lake [...]
> —Luke 8:33 KJV

WEIRD KENTUCKY

The Bell Witch? Old Kate? Bae Bae? Whatever the nomencla-
ture, this "Queen Mab of the Mire" is devil all the same. She has
summoned to herself a maelstrom of centuries-old riverdead,
drawn up through the Southern waterways like blood siphoned
backward through the veins.

I recognize the soldier souls of the *S.S. Sultana*. They are
the Union prisoners of war that were burned alive when their
paddle wheeler exploded on their return trip home. Drawn up
the tributaries of the Mississippi River, they have materialized
into a slack-jawed multitude of smoldering skeletons. Together
they sing low in a silent key. And I am completely surrounded.

"You mewlin' sissy," Kate taunts. "Turn out yer pockets and
hand hit over!"

Now I must call upon my years at Fellowship Assembly, sum-
moning the Holy Ghost, walking and talking with God... walking in on exorcisms. I have trained for this day. For this very
moment. So here goes. Faith, don't fail me now!

"I rebuke you in the name of Jesus!" I command, doing my
best to will this thing away.

Indeed, Kate's checkerboard eyeballs bulge at His mere men-
tioning, and the cigarillo suddenly falls from her razor lips. But
after a pause she continues, "How do you know hit ain't He
what sent me?"

I pause. A witch, in league with Christ? I don't think so.

Sensing my reticence, she bares her terrible teeth and
slowly raises her vulture-like claws. At the snap of her fingers, more ghastly forms step forward. I see the Goatman, the

legendary monster from Pope Lick Creek. Then there's Fishhead of Reelfoot Lake. And flickering in and out appears a parade of feedsack-hooded Night Riders sloshing through the marsh on coal black mares. One rider, a bushwhacker, caps a Ball jar of extracted teeth and laughs with a raspy death rattle.

The executed dead from the state pen, I suspect. Cast-offs from the old prison body chute. That's how institutions disposed of bodies in the old days, and why such places were built so close to rivers. They would just slide the dead down a concrete shaft and into the water. Little did the prison guards suspect that they were supplying a direct deposit into the River Styx.

Then what to my wondering eyes appears but the familiar face of my old high school teacher. Brother Withers! I recognize the curve of his harelip in the petrified grain of a cypress trunk. He bends low and woe-begotten like a Jack o' the woods. A beard of bees swarms around his horrified pleading hole. Bless his heart. I reckon it's true. Just like in old Dante's dream: committers of suicide really do come back as trees.

"Dear Jesus, help me!"

MEAT

They say "stars fell on Alabama." That's nice. But meat once rained on Kentucky. True story! And it's happening again. Piles of raw flesh smack the swamp, splat upon the limbs, and land on my head.

For it is written…

> Flesh Descending in a Shower, An Astonishing
> Phenomenon in Kentucky.
> Fresh Meat Like Mutton Falling from a Clear
> Sky.
> On last Friday a shower of meat fell near the
> house of Allen Crouch, who lives some two or

three miles from the Olympia Springs in the southern portion of [Bath] County, covering a strip of ground about one hundred yards in length and fifty wide. [...] [Mrs. Crouch] said it fell like large snowflakes [...] One piece fell near her which was three or four inches square. Mr. Harrison Gill, whose veracity is unquestionable, [...] hearing of this occurrence visited the locality the next day, and says he saw particles of meat sticking to the fences and scattered over the ground. The meat when it first fell appeared to be perfectly fresh. Two gentlemen, who tasted the meat, express the opinion that it was either mutton or venison.

—*New York Times*, March 10, 1876

But above it all, stretching from due east to due west is the looming skyscape of an angry great spirit. His arms are out-held like Christ. However, I sense his intentions are anything but Christ-like. It appears he is the one directing this moment like a grand puppeteer. In each fist he grips the weft and the warp of space-time in curling strands.

My head rolls back on my neck as Old Kate's gap-toothed goblins gather up the pulp of my dying body. Fain to resist, I'm soon set back on my feet and scourged forth by the Night Riders. The *Sultana* soldiers hold their bayonets on me and off I'm driven, paraded through the netherglades, past the other lost souls trapped as trees. Before long I am lashed to a gnarly dead oak. The POWs and Night Riders form a gunpoint circle around me as the Bell Witch shoulders herself through for one last assault.

"Haw Haw Haww-w!" goes her crackle. "Now where's th' Stone?"

"Huh?"

"If ye hain't got the Mad Stone, who does?"

"Mad Stone? If I had that I would've already dealt with this snakebite, and I sure as hell wouldn't be dealing with you!"

"Everwhat ye want!" Kate cries, raising both sets of talons with a maestro's flourish. A Brueghel-esque scene of revelry erupts. Her minions commence to celebrate with crooked fiddle tunes and ghoulish double-time dancing, like the fast-motion footage of a lost silent film. My only comfort now is the drone I've heard all my life. Comfort in knowing that I was right and Carver was wrong. The sound definitely comes from the trees. It is the ghostly moan of Hell's choir blasting up from yawning wooden chambers. As if in celebration that Hell is currently reigning on Earth.

MEDUSA

Kate produces a budding young sapling of the infamous Kudzu kind. Her grasp loosens and down it plops into the swamp. Upon impact, the depths begin to bubble and roil. Soon all of Clarks River and its tributaries, as far as the eye can see, become a churning cesspool, dredging up the filthiest, utmost dregs from the bottoms. Green gunk, sewage, and sediment rise to the top, and in an instant, a leafy flourish explodes from the waters. Like the snakes of a caduceus, they wrap me head to toe and lift. I plead for mercy but Kate and company vanish in a blue flash of foxfire.

Likewise, I am in transit, intertwined with The Vine That Ate The South. Up, up, and up! Like a beanstalk in a Jack tale. Away into the pinetops, I am gathered by its tentacles. Now it is I who will feel the fate of my long-sought prize, the dead lovers of the Kudzu House of Horrors. My morbid curiosity. My fascination with my homeland. My need to be adventurous. It's got me nowhere nearer to that for which I was searching. I might as well have stayed at home.

But wait! I spoke too soon. They are right here. Right beside me! The dead husband and his wife, flanking me like thieves on the cross. We are all three displayed in a gothic Golgotha of bones and Kudzu, pitched high as the steepled tent of the Devil's circus. Tight wires and trapezes, nets and rope, as if all tangled by a twister. Tangled like the chicken scratch of Satan's own signature. Our bodies must forever hover together here now, woven in Kudzu, the three of us, lashed as Mazeppa and stitched into infinite density. A breeze clonks the old man's skull against the tree, like a head hits hard on the timbers of a pall-borne coffin. His brow is tethered by the dry, dead tendrils of his Caesarian laurel... a loose yo-yoing leash of ivy that keeps letting his head knock and recoil in the wind.

And she is just hanging here horrified.

"If thou be our lone savior, why dost thou not save thyself?" he asks.

But the other, answering, rebukes him, saying, 'Dost thou not even fear God, seeing thou art under the same condemnation? And thou and I indeed justly, for we receive the due reward of our hermitage; but this boy hath done nothing wrong."

Then he turns his skull to say unto me, "Boy, remember us to the world if thou returneth to thy people."

In turn I reply, "Varily, I say, today thou shalt be in Paradise."

O such indignity! But at least Stoney Kingston's tag is nowhere to be seen on the tree. At least, as far as I can see, he is a liar. Plus I am their "lone savior"! At least there's that.

The floodwaters below are but a glistening glass-bottom, reflecting a sentinel of rising stars. I can barely take in air, trapped between thick rustling leaves and the bulging veins of the purple-plumed Lobed Mountain Child.

Woe is me, I am undone. I am, at long last, abandoned in a delirium to ponder my slow supernatural homicide. My untimely demise.

ALOFT

From my treetop loft, I hear the clacking fan blades of Old Man Demp's windmill. It's not the kind of windmill that siphons up water for cattle. It's the kind that drills an annoying noise into the earth to scare away the gophers and moles. I can hear pie tins rattling in his garden too. All sounds meant to frighten off living things. I imagine the furrows of his farm to be the shallow graves of his many victims, buried lengthwise, head-to-toe and row after row.

There are signs of civilization though, each one a strange, mild comfort in my final moments: the dusty high beams of a combine working into the night, the vesper bells of Fellowship Assembly, a cumulus of steam from the coal plant, drifting contrails set alive by the receding sunset, and the red beacons of distant phone towers, whose signals are useless here. They pulse on and off, almost in mockery.

My spirit jumps with the phantom gestures that come with claustrophobia, like a baby chick trying to muscle out of its shell. Please, God. I want to be free again to savor each of life's little freedoms. Rescue or death, hell or high water, free me from this Kentucky crucifixion. Hear my message. Send it forth! Spark my teeth!

Although struggling in the last moments of life, I can make out the sweeping light from a nearby airstrip. My fading eyesight follows the swirling beam as it alternates blue and white, cutting the night into moonbow rings.

REVENGE OF THE SIN EATER

But, I am quickly sickened as the light strikes the face of Dooney on his treetop plank just yards away. Grinnin' like a possum eatin' peach seeds, he can clearly see me struggling like a tangled marionette. Still he squats on the balls of his feet, arms extended straight between his bent knees, wristbones touching, and toting a rifle that lies flat across his forearms. He is a tow-headed troll of a man; an Ed Gein doppelganger, with a jacked-up face, gin blossoms, and a cauliflower bulb for a nose. He dons a flannel hunting cap with the flaps snapped up, revealing equally cauliflowered ears. I put him around 40, 42-ish. And though supposedly mute, he can be heard speaking.

"Grin-deddy sed 'git.'"

"Excuse me?"

"He tole me t'kep these here hwoods clur. This is Burkeholder land."

Reader, there can be few depths lower than spending your last moments on Earth with a gun-totin', wall-eyed inbreed. But perhaps this one can be reasoned with. I take a deep breath and give'r a go. "Look. Dooney, right? Please. Help me down. Cut me down and I promise I, we, will never come back. I am so, so sorry. Please tell your grandfather we're sorry and we'll never ever ever come back."

"Grin-deddy is wipf Jeeziff now, but he's all het up 'n done tole you git."

"Dooney, look, I need a doctor. I've got bit by a snake and I, I need to get down from here, okay? I'm having a hard time. I'm losing it and I think the poison is, uh, making me crazy. Affecting me in a bad way. Can you run go get a doctor? Somebody needs to come cut me down from here, okay?"

"Nuh-uh. Ah ain't." Dooney cocks his rifle and aims it between my eyes.

"No no no no no! Don't shoot! You don't want that. You

don't need that kind of trouble. What if all your church friends find out? They wouldn't be nice to you anymore, right?"

"Ah hain't a-gerna shoot ye, but ah orta." He pauses for a second.

"Yep. Ah orta. No. Ah'll let them vines thar do th' trick, in stid. That's Grin-deddy's hway o' doin' hit. Them's is his hands!"

With those words I feel the hands, no, the very vice grip of Burkeholder's Deadening strengthen around my ribcage, squeezing my eyeballs nearly out of their sockets. His capillaries surge with sap, swelling the foliage to damn near crush my windpipe. And pop! I just felt a rib give.

Through tears of agony I finally see Dooney for the cursed progeny he is inside. He's not just some homeless, glue-huffing man-child. He's the Sin Eater from the corner of my mind. He is a monstrous, skeletal wretch with fish gills and webbing. An effigy brought to life by woodland hoodoo, hammered together by a pitiless tinker and left to fester in his sores and sin. He is part Judas, part Cain, part walkingstick insect, with crooked crucifix and gravebeam bones that bend backward on rusty hinges… and he is no friend of mine.

SEARCHLIGHTS

At this moment a crop-duster buzzes overhead. It's a search plane, panning its spotlight on us. Its refreshing light sweeps over me in the cool of the evening. I can't believe it. I've been spared! Slow descending flares streak down the firmament like golden tears. Hallelujah! Maybe they've already found Carver too. Oh, praise the LORD, I am saved!

"Oh thank God. I can't wait to tell Delilah the news. I made it and lived to tell the tale!"

I sigh with relief while trying to signal the plane with my tautly wound limbs. Thank goodness. Maybe they picked up the signal I've been trying to transmit from my molars.

"Nuh-uh. Y'aint saved. Cain't nobody cross Grin-deddy. What we do wipf trestpasters is none've ther nevermind. Looka-hure now."

Dooney takes up his rifle and aims it at the small craft's engine. The gun barrel moves in a figure eight, finding its mark until *CRACK*! The shot jerks a knot into the night. And it's a dead hit. The plane sputters and chokes as Dooney bleats a giddy "Squeeeeee!" All at once the craft is sent whirly-birding into a field like a tinkertoy, search-beam and taillights spinning in plaits of sad brilliance.

"Dammit, Dooney. Why'd you have to go and do that?"

"Nighty-night," he says. And with that, my destruction comes at once.

Constricted by a calligraphy of vines, I scream in silence as ten thousand creepers take their course. Prodding and probing, tangling and strangling, looping and interlacing. They worm themselves into every orifice, sinus, and sinew, filling my throat and lungs with bitter unfurling leaves and popping bones with dull thuds. Now they're pushing out my eyeballs, probing their feelers between the creases of my brains and braiding themselves into a masterpiece of arabesque. My soul looks down from its kite string, singing out to anyone so inclined to listen: "Remember me! Know my story!" Let my dental work fire a message to the outside world. A faint signal into the void.

Dooney shimmies down the tree into nothingness. And with that, I soon pass away into a dreamless sleep on a moonless night. The way I'd always imagined death to feel like. Kind of tingly…

EDGAR CAYCE, the "Sleeping Prophet," was born downriver in Beverly, Kentucky, circa 1877. Edgar began experiencing paranormal phenomena as a child, complete with his own "imaginary" spirit friends. As a young adult, he was invited to

become an Ascended Master by St. Germain, who, I may or may not misremember, motioned to him from inside a painting that hung in Cayce's den. He joined the spirit by the hand, stepped into the frame, like Alice through the looking glass, and walked into a secret garden to discuss the mysteries of life.

Cloistered in the lush brushstroke foliage, Edgar was shown the future: the rise of Hitler, the atom bomb, the Kennedy assassination, the World Trade Center attack, and other global events. Later, as his powers grew, he would relay this information from his dream state to a bedside associate who would then publish his prophecies. As a result, Edgar Cayce became our own "Southern Nostradamus." And, although he communed with spirits, he was still accepted as a devout God-fearing member of his local church.

Occultists like these believe true wisdom can be gained by exiting the body to enter an astral plane. They say there is a "golden rope" that kite-strings your body to your soul, to your solar plexus. (It seems I can attest to this. I am here now, dangling by such a thread. And it's good to know that we still hang on for a while after death.) But we must beware; the cord could be cut! Perpendicular "soul traffic" could disconnect us from our power source: those faint electrical pulses that remain in our brain, and we will die all the way.

Of course, you may disregard if you think this is just a load of crap. That this whole episode is a mere figment of my imagination in the deep throes of REM. Hey, I hope you're right! I hope I am at rest somewhere right now, having one hell of a nightmare. Perhaps it's all just the result of that snakebite. If not, then maybe it's just a bad case of indigestion, the result of a rare bit of meat or expired milk. Come to think of it, if the skeptical reader is correct, perhaps all Edgar Cayce needed was a big ol' swig of Pepto-Bismol.

Chapter Twenty-Three
WHITTLE STICK

A stream-of-consciousness litany of regrets.

For all my bellyaching about being babied by my mother and bullied by my schoolmates, all my whining about Daddy, all my carrying on about my rivals in love and waxing poetic about death, I am now left alone to reconsider. In all honesty, I would have preferred to live long enough to become an old man. A classic elderly gentleman with stories to tell. I always thought that growing old and dying was one of the coolest things I'd ever get to do. And not to become a legend necessarily, either. I'd be content as just another forgotten story in the dusty annals kept in a musty, dark room. Let me blur in with all the other worried faces of a crumbling photo album. Or set me alongside those Melungeons I saw peering out through the cataracts of their cameos. I, too, want to be a part of that ever-fading eternal mystery. To be forgotten means your story is too rich to occupy the minds of the madding crowd. Had I lived though, I would have manned up over time, matured, married Delilah, had a family, maybe even some grandkids. But before settling down, perhaps I had done a little living… maybe some traveling. Or better yet, as long as we're making stuff up, maybe I was forced to leave, driven out of Kentucky. Maybe I had gotten into trouble. Was it because I'd fallen in with the wrong crowd? Some shady cast of characters? Maybe we had a secret club. Perhaps you've heard of a certain group called the Honorable Order of Kentucky Colonels, that charitable organization of Southern gents in string ties. Well, maybe we called ourselves the "Dishonorable Order of Kentucky Colonels," a secret society of my own design. We would've been far more interesting than those normal Kentucky Colonels. We would've been mystic oddfellow Kentuckians; we would have held underground meetings just like the Freemasons do. Perhaps we would've even been their rivals! We would've donned drape jackets and string ties in the opposite color scheme of Colonel Sanders. Black suits and white ties! And instead of chicken, we ate CATFISH! Blasphemy! Maybe we would have risen up and loudly made our presence known to the city at large. Maybe we would've crashed the local Christmas parade, joined in the march and beat our drums to recruit other dark souls. Uh-oh! Well now. Having said that, it suddenly looks like it's time to split, as the city leaders are grumbling and the townspeople are revolting. And they are truly revolting. So next I would've run off to, um, join the Merchant Marines! Or maybe I just signed up with the Tuna Fleet. Upon gaining my sea legs and mastering the art of knot-tying, deck-swabbing, and sailing, I would've become a grizzled old tar. A salty dog. Aye, a veritable Poopdeck Pappy! Lean, mean, scrappy, and packin' many a tall tale to regale my future grandchildren. They would hear my harrowing yarns of circumnavigation around Tierra del Fuego and the Horn of Africa, all aboard my mighty ship, the *S.S. Krakatoa*. Well, the *Krakatoa* would be more of a dinghy than a schooner, but boy, if that boat could talk! She would sing of having delivered me deep into far-flung, exotic locales whereupon I did such things as, oh I don't know... lounge with pygmies beneath the flame trees of the Dark Continent, or entertain the crowned heads of Europe with my trusty French harp, or maybe I just laid about, shooting the breeze with the Red Chinese. When the coast was clear, I would've returned from my exploits to a restored Kentucky citizenship. Now they would call me "Colonel," not "Crap Knife." I am a man to be respected! And there, as an old adorable saw, I would one day entertain those many grandchildren of mine, as they sat on the old porch planks of home, gathered about the boots of their elder silver-haired badass. I would hold them spellbound, creaking in my hand-hewn rocking chair, embellishing each tale with colorful asides and lie-after-lie! And whittling all the while. Yes, whittling! Whittling the ivory of a narwhal tusk down to a long slender stick, gliding my Case knife while shavings fall into their smiling eyelashes. Then they would watch as I'd etch a scrimshaw timeline. Little vignettes of each scene I just described, carefully carved in detail. But whoops... upsy daisy! Out to the fencerow I must hobble, old man that I am, after all. I don't move as quick as I used to. I'm all stove up and plum give out. But off I go nonetheless, over to the dewberry bushes to gather berries for ink. I'd squeeze their juices into a rusty Folgers coffee can, carefully daub the ink into each carving, and wipe away the excess. "This will make a fine keepsake for my landlubber grandchildren," I'd say aloud. Ha-wharf! There's that pesky blood-wet rattle in my lungs again, the result of my ever-present corncob pipe. But if it's one thing the sea has taught me, it's that a man must live or die on his own terms. Not just wither away! A captain goes down with the ship! So into the *S.S. Krakatoa* I'd climb. She would be moored on Kentucky's Clarks River, a short walk from the old porch planks of home. I'd be careful to sneak the 12-guage in with my bundle of oars and tackle. And, of course, my whittle stick of ivory. Notched at the base, she would be conveniently just long enough to trip the trigger. Barrel in mouth, the deed would be done, and the whittle stick would fall safely into the hull. It's an excellent heirloom, after all, engraved even with this final scene of suicide, and summing up a triumphant life well spent. The last thoughts of a soul held taut at the end of a kite string.

Chapter Twenty-Four
MOTH MAN

Salvation.
A supernatural stranger.
The "White Thing" appears.

I am snapped-to by a gauntlet of slapping branches. A body-flop into the floodwaters brings me straight awake, and I'm gulping down the green gunk and dredged filth of the creek, coughing it up and having to dog-paddle with one arm. My other arm is still dead, blackened and tight in its tourniquet. And here I am again, chest-deep a-bobbin' in the swollen swampland. I must have shrugged off and coughed up the limp cables that'd held me.

Alert and panicked, at least I can now be free to focus... focus on my next vision, as the bumblebee-swarm of TV static assembles a new picture into place:

COLD

Red veins beat across a charcoal moon. Black as a habit, He appears through a mist of foxfire with ruby eyes. They are as red, round, and wide as bicycle reflectors, and they are positioned where the areolas of man's trunk would be. His head is his torso. His torso is his head.

Despite confounding anatomy, his countenance is immaculate. Lord High Potentate of the Great White Brotherhood! Grand Imperator of the Golden Dawn! With outstretched sable wings, he stands ten feet tall and bulletproof, hovering above the surface of the water and mounds of rained-down meat. He is lean and chiseled, like the body pried off a crucifix. His aura sparkles with a thousand blessings and there is a Shekinah glow that could convert any atheist. Yes, that could whiten the very hairs of Hitchens!

He hums to me with velvet thoughts:

"Rise, ditchling. RISE."

Somehow I know Him by many names. He is Mahatma, Melchizedek, Indrid Cold… three figures found in my father's old leather-bound bestiary of demi-gods. The Ascended Masters. Just as much a myth as the Bell Witch, he is also every bit the matter of official public record:

> And this man stood there, and he first asked me what I was called, and I knew he meant my name. […] And then he asked me, he said 'Why are you frightened?' He said 'Don't be frightened, we wish you no harm.' He said […] 'We wish you only happiness.' And I told him my name, and when I told him my name, he said He was called 'Cold.' That was the name that he was called by.
>
> —Woodrow Wilson Derenberger interview,
> WTAP-TV, November 2, 1966.

He appeared as both a "Grinning Man" and a "Mothman" to the good people of Point Pleasant, West Virginia, in the 1960s, foretelling of a bridge collapse. Perhaps, like the other spirits,

He has traveled here through water, from the confluence of the Kanawha and Ohio Rivers. Or maybe he just flew. He is the Mothman, after all.

They say Hell hath its demons and Heaven hath its angels, but whatever weird Purgatory I'm trapped in now hosts its own cast of characters. Mr. Cold's friend, the White Thing, is just as Carver had described it: a four-foot-tall panther standing on its back legs and always out of reach some fifty feet away. And again, just as Carver described, it sings past its fangs with the voice of a crying child.

Though in the presence of the highest of Masonic gods, obeisance is an afterthought. Relief to be alive comes first! I recall my escape. A loosening from my leafy death-grip, followed by a 100-foot plummet into the swamp.

"You are safe and I am 'COLD,'" came his voice like a sonic boom. I beg for pardon and any explanation as to what was happening. Am I really alive? Where is the witch and all her gap-toothed cave-goblins?

And what about the Night Riders, the *Sultana* soldiers, and all the old, dead prisoners? What is it that they want from me? Why was I set free? Am I safe now?

"What do you remember?" Mr. Cold asks, his thundering voice rippling the sludge.

"I-I remember gasping for air... sir. I was choked by the ivy and I fell asleep. A sleep sounder than death. Then, well... I felt like I was flying! There was the sensation of flight."

"Go on."

"I could feel a cold wind in my face and the sense of weightlessness. I opened my eyes and, yes, I was flying... way on up, way up in the stratosphere! But my mind was always scanning the woods, much lower to the ground, like a hawk hunting mice. I was in search of someone."

"You are the one who is lost," Cold sternly states.

"Yes, sir. But there were two of us. I was looking for my

friend… Carver. He was my guide out here. But he had to turn around."

"You should have both turned around miles ago." The odd god's eyes throb with a pulse of fire. The White Thing intones his infamous dark idylls, singing quietly in the background.

I continue talking nervously to avoid further scorn. "Um, well. He went back to wash off in the creek. But I found him much, much farther back. I could see him scrambling up onto that old man's property. Old Man Demp. Do you know the man? Gray flattop, navy blue coveralls, gold spray-painted boots. He hates trespassers."

I struggle to recall more details.

"Carver went back to help someone. No, it was to save something.

Yes! I remember. His uncle's old broke-down racehorse! It had wandered onto private property and this Demp fellow took a notion to kill it. And not just to shoot it but to string it up… you know, like to hang it… with a noose… like they used to do to people. Carver must have seen him from the creek, trying to lynch that horse, so he ran up the bluff to stop him. All I know is that they got into a scuffle and it didn't end well. Next thing I saw was Uncle Earl's racehorse dangling by a rope off the cliff, kicking its hind legs. Then Carver… while he was trying to pull it in and cut it loose he… he got shot in the gut! Oh Jesus."

It dawns on me. Carver is lying up there on a bluff beneath a carpet of Kudzu, completely hidden from view. My voice swells with grief.

"Ah, Carver Canute," Cold muses, "a mighty oak has fallen."

"Oh yeah. And how could I forget!? Above it all, I remember, was this giant character gazing down… like some great spirit in the sky. He looked like some Native American chief or a shaman of sorts? Who was that?! He must have taken up the entire sky!"

Mr. Cold exchanges glances with the White Thing and I am instructed to make myself comfortable, as comfortable as one can be when chest-deep sludge is lapping at your throat and your friend is lying dead a mile away. But I am powerless to resist as the Mothman winds up for a tale about this Great Spirit.

LORD, when oh when will story-time be over?

Chapter Twenty-Five
THE CURSE OF COPPERHEAD

Indrid Cold reveals the hidden history of my homeland.

"Picture it: Within the speckled black canvas of endless night, the architects of Fate lie dormant. God and the Devil, locked in stalemate... neither is watching. But there is one other player in this eternal drama. In case you didn't know, the 'Spirit' you saw goes by the name 'Copperhead.' He joined the heavenly Host after he and his tribe of Chickasaw were slaughtered in the skirmishes following the Louisiana Purchase. Copperhead was grandfathered into Heaven to create a more diverse heavenly populace—one not so overwhelmed with Judeo-Christian fuddy-duddies. But do not speak his name lightly, for he is my worst rival. For two hundred years he has whiled away his celestial free time by meting out wickedness from Heaven upon the various nations of white men.

"Then, in the same way one might choose a random location by pelting a finger onto a spinning globe, Copperhead sent his red talon descending through the Chaos to find another area to torment. And all the while, I must add, the hosts of Heaven never suspected a thing.

"Your particular little county is where his finger most

recently fell, almost thirty years ago to the day. His presence was felt within seconds as the townsfolk buckled under his sway. Writhing with misery, malaise, and decay, this place, this "Realm of the Red Snake," helplessly wheeled in his shadow. And he would show no mercy. He never shows mercy.

"When the floods came, your famous Indian burial mounds collapsed: their loose flint and pottery, a flotsam of history. Set free at last were the restless native specters, moving now like mystic swirls along the water, where spirits forever prefer to be. The ground was left a sloshy gray sponge. Cypress knees poked out of the quagmire like wooden shark fins, and what trees remained stood gutted and slumped, depressed that destruction hung so near.

"April flooding subsided as May came pouting in. Receding floodwaters revealed random waterlogged carcasses in the creek beds. The membranous beatings of cicada wings hummed in the gray skies above. They barnstormed the town in an endless onslaught. Pre-war brick facades and blacktop swelled and popped in the ruthless white heat. Branches raked upward like pleading hands. The racket of buzzards and dirt daubers replaced the songs of doves and gulls. The whole county felt like a bee sting. But it wasn't just a change in the weather; it was a shift in attitudes too. Hapless souls, suddenly made slaves to technology, greed, and progress, fell prey to the seven deadly sins. Community spirit was destroyed as families and friends turned inward to nurture their own 'inner child.' Outside the ruins of the town square, plastic backlit signage with fast food logos blazed across the once-lazy horse pastures. Cars honked, charged, and crunched as Copperhead's sacro-savage influence was felt on every level imaginable.

"However, so gradual was the full transformation that no one could quite detect it, although there were signs and signifiers. Locusts emitted a non-stop telemetric chatter, and bleak prophecies were constantly droning through the woodlands.

Tree rings spun like decoder rings ciphering a mystic mathematics. However, some folks read the portents wrong, like Brother Stiles, your local televangelist. Only a chosen few, like the gravekeeper you saw today, could read the signs correctly.

"Regardless, Copperhead continued to pull no punches ushering in this new Dark Age, this 'Age of Information.'

"'You want progress?' he said. 'I'll give you progress!'

"What brain cells were spared by the television were fried by the even flashier technology. And don't get me started on what they put in the tap water! Suffice to say, it was all one tacky headlong rush into extreme industry and leisure, and its consequences were felt full force. Enslaved by marketing and poisoned by processed foods and pharmaceuticals, the living were now dead, dead on the inside, and the actual dead didn't know how good they had it."

I am still in a daze of swarming dots and droning woods, trying to understand who these entities are—Mr. Indrid Cold, the White Thing, and Copperhead—and what they want with me. Regardless, the Mothman continues recounting the hidden history of my homeland:

"Indeed, just when you'd think it couldn't get any worse, none other than Saint Gabriel himself—in a *flash!*—wrestled the 'Red Snake' from his post and cast him from Heaven. It was an explosive maelstrom of fury and Copperhead was at last doomed, his deeds exposed and his schemes upended. His wings were sawn off by Saint Joseph, the patron saint of carpenters, and, just like Lucifer who was banished in a bolt of lightning, Copperhead suffered the same electric justice. The Van Allen belt snapped the dark voltage earthward, and within the blink of an eye, the Southern landscape below became the recipient of its own tormentor. With a deafening crack of thunder, his spirit struck directly into the heart of Marshall County.

"But rather than being driven into the ground and on into Hell, the lightning bolt unfortunately arced. It struck a pole. Yes, a literal iron flagpole. The surge followed along a connecting metal leash and zapped a path straight into a chained-up junkyard dog. Yes, son. Right into the very soul of a certain German Shepherd."

"'Sparky,'" chimed the White Thing from fifty feet away.

"Yes. Sparky is the name of this animal, ironically..." Cold continues.

"Probably not the same 'Sparky' with brass balls," I somehow muse to myself.

"The fur ran white down the hackles of the cursed cur's back, his eyes clouded over with evil. Then, around the pole, the hainted hound did run, night and day, until the yard became a muddy circle of dog tracks and rabid foam.

"However, while Copperhead seethed inside his new canine confines, something amazing happened. Something miraculous. For just as a human heart can be defibrillated by an electric charge, the heart of your homeland was released from its sickness and energized with fresh new power. A couple of Walmarts caught fire, the Lowes closed down, and folks started waking up out of their comas of self-absorption.

"The evil rush to progress had been abated and everything immediately went back to near-normal.

"What you will find even more interesting is that this all just happened mere moments ago, the exact moment when you were sent splashing to freedom. Your vines loosened, your tree was felled, and the Bell Witch was sent screaming back to her cave in Tennessee.

"But, be warned. This good news only lasts as long as Copperhead is held hostage within the soul of another living thing. So, for the sake of your family and friends, you had better pray to God that dog keeps running."

"So we're safe for now... sir?" I ask, remembering my place.

St. Joseph saws the wings off Copperhead

"Yes, you are safe for now. As long as that dog is alive, which he is. Beyond that, I cannot tell. It is up to the LORD."

"But what's this business with the Mad Stone? Kate said she wanted me to hand it over. But Carver's got it."

"Your friend is carrying something special. It is one of only five in existence. Together they are powerful..." he pauses. "As your father once knew."

"You knew my dad?" I ask, still bobbing in the muck in disbelief.

"We can do better than that!" he says, motioning toward the White Thing.

"My friend can sing it to you."

Chapter Twenty-Six
THE ORDER OF COPPERHEAD

The White Thing sings.
Cult activity.
The story of my father revealed.

The White Thing is a curious creature. Not as odd as a Mothman, a Bell Witch, a Sin Eater, or a forest of dead souls, but still quite bizarre. There is a Cheshire cat quality to him, an aloof translucence. There is also a tangible, sinewy aspect to this half-real beast, and a musculature that is 100 percent pure Kentucky panther. His fur is light gray, dull, and matted. He throws no shadow but is himself a pale penumbra of another world: a world "east of the sun and west of the moon."

His voice is banshee-high, clarion and sad, and the tale he sings spells out the occult backstory of my father's dealings with something called the "Order of Copperhead."

Perhaps it must be added to the litany of other secret societies found deep in the backwoods South, the ones I mentioned before: the Ku Klux Klan, the Night Riders, the Loyal Leagues, the Rifle Clubs, and the Red Shirts. Not to mention the Order of Myths, the Mardi Gras marauders of Joe Cain.

The White Thing stands erect, facing away with his paws held behind his back and his chest swelled up like a diplomat. His song of satanic conspiracy begins:

Way down south
In a Ken-Tuck town
Where all of the Stubblefields grow
One man did rise
With the Devil in his eyes
Whose heart was dark as West Field coal.
Heart was dark as West Field coal.

Twelve angry men
Did join him in his sins.
They knelt around a darkened grave.
They drew their daggers down,
The red ran to the ground
And they licked along the bloodied blades.
They licked along the bloodied blades.

He said that he would share
His sacrificial heir
As soon as the child could be bred.
They swore a bloody oath
And drank a bloody toast
And called themselves the Order of Copperhead
Called themselves the Order of Copperhead

When that awful day did come
To offer up his son,
He hid his only heir far from home.
But the Order did give chase
To hunt both night and day,
While the father sought the five Mad Stones.
He did search for the five magic stones.

Only four of the stones
Were able to be loaned,
A fifth one would remain hid.
But with four well in the hand
T'was plenty to command
A war against the cult of Copperhead.
War against the cult of Copperhead.

Years did come and go
When at last one golden dawn,
The men did meet to battle to the death.
But the father, he was felled
So too the fearsome Twelve
Yet an evil prayer escaped their dying breath.
A prayer escaped the Order's dying breath.

"Copperhead" is the name
Of their shaman god of pain,
Chief among the devils of the dead.
"Of stones, there is a fifth
Hidden with his kith,
Avenge us!" they called to Copperhead.
And so died the Order of Copperhead.

Copperhead, in his rage,
Commenced an evil Age
To lure the son into his watchful woods.
Yes, the heir and his friend
Were to meet a fatal end,
But the LORD God is just and is good.
And smote the Serpent rightly where he stood.

Take heed all ye wandering children so lost!
Dwell not in the caves of your mind.
Though the sins of the father
Are paid upon the son
His love is revealed over time
A father's love is revealed in time.

The refrain hits me hard. I'm both devastated with relief and flabbergasted beyond belief. My wicked father, redeemed now to a degree, at last had enough humanity to sacrifice his own life in order to save mine. But what possessed him to get involved with such darkness in the first place? To hold court with a cult and promise to offer me, his infant child, as human sacrifice? What the hell?

Was it easier for him to prove the existence of the Devil than God? Or was it just more fun?

But by forming this pagan "Copperhead" group my father had bitten off more than he could chew. Initially it gave him power, a power that perhaps flourished in The Deadening. But it wasn't enough to help him withstand the wages of his own sin.

It occurs to me, as the two gods blur from view: I have now been spared twice, once by my terrestrial father and again by my Heavenly Father. If somewhere on my deathbed I am having this dream, indeed if I am receiving this message, then I am content to let go of my kite string and float off to meet my Maker. I have been blessed with a new comforting knowledge, a perspective that could only be provided in a fugue state. I am ready to be turned loose now, like so many shiny red balloons from the Kansas State Fair.

Chapter Twenty-Seven
GALLAVANT'S END

Resuscitation.
Carver Canute's fate.
Epilogue.

Dear Mother,
    I am dead.
    I loved you though. Remember in church? Halfway through the sermon, when you'd tear a stick of mint gum in half and we'd share? I loved that.
    I hope I see you one day.

mint... Mint... MINT
Like its cousin "seafoam green," the color "mint" reminds us of tropical havanas, shady seclusion, and safe harbor. It was a popular color in the 1950s, with everything from kitchen appliances to automobiles sporting the hue of the Hawaiian tropics (their new fiftieth state!). It is what doctors preferred to paint their operating rooms too. This is not just due to mid-century modern aesthetics. Rather, mint green is the natural complement of blood red. And as such, it neutralizes the after-image

that imprints upon the surgeon's retina during long hours of muck-raking and bone-sawing. Any other color and he would still see spots.

So if you were to ask me what color symbolizes virtue I would tell you that mint is infinitely better than the classic answer, white. After all, mint is the color God Himself chose to negate the visual sting of blood, not to mention man's age-old enemy, Fire!

Mint is also the calming lens through which I observe my new life... the color of these hospital walls. And it is the polar opposite of the bloody veil that has been the back of my eyelids for what seems months on end.

Photons of light assemble. The pixels of life! Suddenly I can see, hear, and feel my surroundings: Mint green walls, a beeping EKG monitor, a flat-screen TV, an overhead bulb, papery sheets, and painful plastic tubing. But my first instinct isn't to yawn, stretch, and take a deep breath. It is to shut that damn TV off! Because if it's one thing I can't stand it's those damn white-trash daytime talk shows, with all their paternity tests, food fights, and the hypocritical "moral" at the end from the host.

I lunge for the remote control that sits an arm's length away on my bedside tray, but I strangely come up short. An "arm's length" is precisely what I'm lacking.

"Oh no! They cut my arm off!" I gasp. "Oh God, no."

I reckon there's been about two days' worth of missing time since I discovered the amputation. I vaguely remember waking up once to discover a photo of myself taped to a coffee can full of money from my old pals at the drugstore. There were also a few Xeroxed copies of *The Orthopaedics Journal* set in a stack next to my bed. "Surviving a Snakebite" and "Starting Over As an Amputee" were the stories stapled in the corner and left for me to read. There was a picture of an Iraqi War soldier on one, I want to say. Then, it seems, a doctor might have come in and talked to me about my allergic predisposition to… blah blah blah. Something about a copperhead bite.

To make matters worse, my current state of depression and pain is only compounded by my new visitor, Skitch Canute. The Devil's understudy, always ready and willing to fill in in a pinch.

"What were you two fudge-packers doin' runnin' around in the woods anyway?" Skitch yells from the hallway as he strides into the room. Strutting in like he runs the place.

"Where's your brother? Where's Carver?" I ask, mustering the strength to deal with this jerk. Skitch is only loud like this when he knows it will annoy someone.

"He's on the other side of the damn room, Sherlock, if ya just turn yer head and look."

Sure enough, Carver is lying in the bed next to mine. He is purpled and swollen beyond recognition. A hose has been fed down his throat. I see his heart rate on the EKG. It limps along like a three-legged dog.

"Is he gonna pull through?"

"Yeah. They found him just in time, thanks to that dogpath ol' Tabitha Holt's been cuttin' out there. It made for quick n' easy access."

"How? I mean, how did they find him? How did they know where to even start?"

"After y'all come up missin' fer so long, they finally sent out a search plane. The government keeps a fleet of crop dusters over at the waterworks. But somebody shot one th' damn thangs down. It was that Dooney dumbass if I had t'guess. They sent some church folks down the dogpath to comb through that patch and they heard a bell a-ringin'.

"Turns out that old 'Bell'd Buzzard' o' mine was circlin' Carver's half-dead carcass. They never did find the plane's pilot though, so it was really a lucky break that they found ol' numb-nuts here, I tell ya what. They's no way they woulda found him hidden up under all that laurel hell if it haint been for that bird looking for dinner."

"How long were we missing?"

"Yessir, it was that Old Man Demp what shot Carver. But looka here. Right before Demp pulled the trigger, good ol' Carver fired off a chunk of concrete and clocked that sum'mitch right between the eyes. Kilt 'im deader'n a dog in a ditch. Hah HA! DIE, you old bastard!" With my remote control, Skitch cranks the volume on today's talk show and leans in for the paternity results.

Delilah and Stoney, plus that Vietnam vet from the FOOD OWL, sit awaiting the announcement from the man in the sweater. The verdict is in: Stoney, that puppet-headed fraud, is the father. And I'm so crushed I can't feel a damn thing. But it's like I don't even care anymore. Really, though. Who needs romance right now when life's biggest question has already been answered? There IS a God!

"Wow," I muster through a fog of woe, swallowing a lump. "Wow…"

"What?"

"Nothing," I sigh. "Nothing at all."

"I wish I coulda seen ol' Carver in action, boy. He always was a dead aim."

"He must've picked him off with that concrete grape he swiped from the graveyard."

"Well, y'all are both lucky as all git out. Hell, they found you wound up in some weeds floatin' face down in a swamp, swoll up with a snakebite. They picked up some faint radio message outta your neck of the woods. Not sure about that though. They're callin' it a miracle. And I don't know if you've noticed or not but they had to whack yer arm off, dude. You musta got a corruption, pukin' up all that blood like ya did. Shoooo! Well, yer mama says she'll be back by later with the doctor. They're gonna put one of them robot hooks on ya. So I reckon you'll hafta get used to beatin' off with the other hand, ha ha!"

Before I pass out again, I catch one last fleeting glimpse of the TV bolted up in the corner of the mint green ceiling. Skitch has flipped it to a 24-hour cable news network. Beneath footage of a smoldering Walmart, today's true date is indicated along the crawl.

Yes, it has been well over 365 days since Carver first kicked that KEEP OUT sign into toothpicks. And, while I may have lost a year—and my One True Love—I must remember that I've gained two other very important things, things a whole lifetime can be spent in search of. I have won both a best friend in Mr. Carver Canute and the perfect father figure in the LORD God Almighty. My father's back-assward quest for God has been attained by the son. For how can such evil run amok on our planet without some sort of balancing force?

Don't get me wrong. It's not like I'm going to join back up with some temple full of moneygrubbing preachers and crackpots. Yeah, I'm content to go it alone, parting the sea of charlatans, townies, meth heads, and trailer brides, and focusing on the positive, especially now that I've run a gauntlet of negativity. I'm too tired to live a life of doubt and darkness. It's just flat out crippling.

Yes, now I must focus, focus, focus. I will meditate on and stand by my new Father. Because, even if God doesn't exist, everybody in the "New South," myself included, would probably be better off going back to thinking that He does.

Chapter Twenty-Eight
CARVER part 2

Dear Jesus. God, if you can hear my monkey ass... Man, I am soooo sorry. I know I done a lot of downright mean things. I've stole a buncha thangs what didn't belong to me. I've done a lot of fornicatin' and drankin'. I even kilt a man or two. Demp, fer one. (Well, I stand by what I done to him. Self-defense, plain as day!) But you know as well as I do that that other feller, he was already deader'n shit. (Pardon my French.) I hope to God (I mean I hope to YOU) that this old boy, lyin' in that other bed right cheer, Crap Knife, never finds out about his daddy and what an asshole he was.

I mean, you saw them that day... all them Santannic weirdos tryin' to kill one another in the woods out there. Goofy buncha fellers, wearin' them funny-lookin' capes. Lookin' as queer as a football bat. And if you ask me, they had to be into some pretty blackish magic or somethin'. Hell, I watched 'em fight for a half an ire. Floatin' in the air like that? I thought I done walked up on a movie shoot! Till I saw all them blood and guts a-blowin' out of 'em.

But, Lawd Lawd, how I knowed that one hurt one in the middle! Ho ho ho! Yessir! Meemaw made me promise to never forget that face. He was a thief, a criminal, a murderer! Hell, they all were. No Mad Stone belongs to any white man. No offense, Jesus. But you know I'm right.

Besides, it was a downright act of mercy, what I done. The mean thang to do woulda been to just let him lay there sufferin'. I did the right thang, even though I didn't report it... though I stashed his body where them Masons might get the blame.

But, the way I see it, I kilt two birds with one stone: I showed him mercy and I ridded the world of one less black-magic asshole. But it ain't like I'm pride of it. It ain't like I don't worry at night thinkin' about it. I know I got a messed-up thrill showin' my buddy his own dead daddy. And I know I'm bound fer hell-far tarnation... where the worm dyeth not.

But, spare me Jesus Christ and I swear I'll get right! No more cussin', screwin', stealin', trestpastin', nothin'! Hell, I'll even start goin' to church again and drag Skitch along! Oh please, please. Please set this Mad Stone to healin' me quick. Right cheer. Right now. Please man. Aw, come on!

Well, wait a minute, buddy. On second thought, hold up! Let's cut the crap. I know you know that I know. That I seed a lot of strange things while lyin' here half-dead. So there ain't no need for us to kid one another or me to keep tryin' to kiss your butt.

So how 'bout this?

If you set me back on the good foot, I'll run over and put that damn dog down. Then I'll get that spirit deep down in my bones... right on down in my soul. Then you and him kin settle this thing face to face, once't and for all. And that orta be one helluva time!

What d'ya say, old man?

The End

ACKNOWLEDGMENTS

This book is dedicated to my wonderful parents, Steve and Linda Wilkes; and to all who bear the Wilkes family name.

Much obliged to the "oral tradition" and to those who have shared stories with me over the years: K. Layne Hendrickson, Jessica Wilkes, Michael Hagaman, Jamie and Katie Barrier, Shooter Jennings, Billy Bob Thornton, Brett Whitacre, Barry Winfield, Lesley Patterson, Keven McQueen, Blake Judd, Jim Joyce, Nathan Blake Lynn, Patty Templeton, Keven McQueen, Keith Holt, Linda and Stephen Wilkes, Steph and Andrea Atnip, Blanca Fiser and Sam "Dreams Don't Chase Themselves" Barrett.

Special mention must also be made of the influence of the late great Southern writers Irvin S. Cobb and John Faulkner.

Thanks also to Eric and Eliza Obenauf for seeing potential in the earlier, written stages of this strange dream.

Two Dollar Radio
Books too loud to Ignore

ALSO AVAILABLE Here are some other titles you might want to dig into.

RADIO IRIS NOVEL BY ANNE-MARIE KINNEY

← "Unexpected and triumphant."
—*New York Times Book Review*

← "'The Office' as scripted by Kafka." —*Star-Tribune*

FOLLOWING A YOUNG RECEPTIONIST, *Radio Iris* deals with watercooler in an artful and existential way, delivering an eerie allegory of the Great Recession.

THE CORRESPONDENCE ARTIST
NOVEL BY BARBARA BROWNING

← "Both witty and devastating." —*Nylon*

AN UNREMARKABLE WOMAN HAS been carrying on with an internationally recognized artist, largely via e-mail. To protect her paramour's identity, she creates a series of correspondent, alternative lovers in a self-destructing roman à clef.

BABY GEISHA STORIES BY TRINIE DALTON

← "Half ingenuous and half wily, winningly hard to pin down. The result is a kind of everyday fantastic." —*Bookforum*

A COLLECTION OF THIRTEEN sexually-charged stories that roam from the Coney Island Ferris wheel to the Greek Isles.

THE ABSOLUTION OF ROBERTO
ACESTES LAING NOVEL BY NICHOLAS ROMBES

← "Kafka directed by David Lynch doesn't even come close." —*3:AM Magazine*

A RARE-FILM LIBRARIAN at a state university in Pennsylvania mysteriously burned his entire stockpile of film canisters and disappeared. Years later, a journalist tracks the forgotten man down to a motel on the fringe of the Wisconsin wilds.

Thank you for supporting independent culture!
Feel good about yourself.

Books to read!

THE ONLY ONES NOVEL BY CAROLA DIBBELL

→ **Best Books 2015:** *Washington Post, O, The Oprah Magazine*, NPR

← "Breathtaking." —NPR

INEZ WANDERS A POST-PANDEMIC world immune to disease. Her life is altered when a grief-stricken mother that hired her to provide genetic material backs out, leaving Inez with the product: a baby girl.

BINARY STAR NOVEL BY SARAH GERARD

→ **Los Angeles Times Book Prize Finalist**

→ **Best Books 2015:** *BuzzFeed, Vanity Fair*, NPR

← "Rhythmic, hallucinatory, yet vivid as crystal." —NPR

AN ELEGIAC, INTENSE PORTRAIT of two young lovers as they battle their personal afflictions while on a road trip across the U.S.

THE REACTIVE NOVEL BY MASANDE NTSHANGA

← "Often teems with a beauty that seems to carry on in front of its glue-huffing wasters despite themselves." —*Slate*

A CLEAR-EYED, COMPASSIONATE ACCOUNT of a young HIV+ man grappling with the sudden death of his brother in South Africa.

THE GLOAMING NOVEL BY MELANIE FINN

→ **New York Times Notable Book of 2016**

← "Deeply satisfying." —*New York Times Book Review*

AFTER AN ACCIDENT LEAVES her estranged in a Swiss town, Pilgrim Jones absconds to east Africa, settling in a Tanzanian outpost where she can't shake the unsettling feeling that she's being followed.

Radio Waves
Visit the blog of Two Dollar Radio, featuring exclusive author interviews, videos, book trailers, and more!

Books to read!

Now available at **TWODOLLARRADIO.com** or your favorite bookseller.

MIRA CORPORA NOVEL BY **JEFF JACKSON**

⇢ **Los Angeles Times Book Prize Finalist**

← "A piercing howl of a book." —*Slate*

A COMING OF AGE story for people who hate coming of age stories, featuring a colony of outcast children, teenage oracles, amusement parks haunted by gibbons, and mysterious cassette tapes.

NOG NOVEL BY **RUDOLPH WURLITZER**

← "[*Nog*'s] combo of Samuel Beckett syntax and hippie-era freakiness mapped out new literary territory for generations to come." —*Time Out New York*

NOG TELLS THE TALE of a man adrift through the American West, armed with nothing more than his own three pencil-thin memories and an octopus in a bathysphere.

THE ORANGE EATS CREEPS
NOVEL BY **GRACE KRILANOVICH**

⇢ **National Book Foundation '5 Under 35' Award**

← "Breathless, scary, and like nothing I've ever read." —NPR

A RUNAWAY SEARCHES FOR her disappeared foster sister along the "Highway That Eats People" haunted by a serial killer named Dactyl.

SQUARE WAVE NOVEL BY **MARK DE SILVA**

← "Compelling and horrifying." —*Chicago Tribune*

A GRAND NOVEL OF ideas and compelling crime mystery, about security states past and present, weather modification science, micro-tonal music, and imperial influences.

SOME RECOMMENDED LOCATIONS FOR READING TWO DOLLAR RADIO BOOKS:

Elevated places, such as hilltops or vineyards. Cafés and wine bars with high spirits. Double-decker buses, planes, hot air balloons, and trees. Or, pretty much anywhere because books are portable and the perfect technology!